P9-DVO-473

MALAFEMMENA

MALAFEMMENA

stories

LOUISA ERMELINO

SARABANDE BOOKS [S] LOUISVILLE, KY

Library of Congress Cataloging-in-Publication Data

Ermelino, Louisa, author.
Malafemmena : stories / Louisa Ermelino.
First edition. | Louisville, KY : Sarabande Books, [2016]
LCCN 2015037229 | ISBN 9781941411292 (softcover : acid-free paper)
BISAC: FICTION / Cultural Heritage.
LCC PS3555.R55 A6 2016 | DDC 813/.54—dc23
LC record available at http://lccn.loc.gov/2015037229

Cover design and interior by Kristen Radtke.

Manufactured in Canada.
This book is printed on acid-free paper.

Sarabande Books is a nonprofit literary organization.

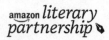

This project is supported in part by an award from the National Endowment for the Arts. The Kentucky
Arts Council, the state arts agency, supports Sarabande Books with state tax dollars and federal funding
from the National Endowment for the Arts.

For the next ones: Lulu, Conrad, Nick, and Joe

TABLE OF CONTENTS

WHERE IT BELONGS

When the baby was born, the mother asked the midwife to take the afterbirth outside.

"I can't," Alfonsina whispered. "You got a girl. Don't you want her to stay home?"

The mother didn't. Armando was somewhere in the streets, already drunk, angry that he'd made a buttonhole.

"Take it outside," the mother said. "This is America."

"I can't," Alfonsina said. "Men go out of the house. No one wants a man who stays home, a *ricchione*, under his mother's skirts. You know that. A woman belongs in the house," she told the mother. "Let me put it down the toilet."

"Take it," the mother said again, "and dig a hole."

Alfonsina looked out the window at the lines of laundry.

"Don't ask me to do this," she said. "I'm too old now. I can't dig a hole so deep the dogs don't find it."

The mother leaned forward. "Take the money from the jar in the kitchen and get someone to help you. Pay them to dig a place and don't say anything."

"But if someone sees?" Alfonsina said. "Everybody knows you got a girl. And Armando? What about Armando?"

Alfonsina pulled a handkerchief from under the sleeve of her dress and twisted it in her fist. The baby cried and the mother turned away.

"Take her," Alfonsina said. "Take your baby and forget this. You got a girl. Girls are always with you. You'll get more babies. You'll get sons."

The mother would not look. She would not take the baby. She would not be persuaded.

"Trouble," Alfonsina said. "You make trouble with this thing, I can tell you."

She went to the kitchen to find the jar. It was behind the tins of flour on the shelf covered in yellow oilcloth.

Alfonsina put the afterbirth in a rag and wrapped it in newspaper. She tied the package with a string. The things people want in America, she thought.

Downstairs in the yard, Alfonsina remembered the baby had no name, and she walked back up the stairs. The mother was sitting at the kitchen table. The sweater over her shoulder had no buttons. She was drinking wine.

"The baby has no name," Alfonsina said.

"Take some wine," the mother said, going to the shelf to get a glass.

"And the baby's name?" Alfonsina said.

"When I go to the priest . . ."

"No," said Alfonsina. "I need it for the legal paper. This is America."

The mother poured the wine. "I don't know."

Alfonsina shook her head. "I come another time, but you don't wait too long. I need it for the paper."

She finished the wine and got up to go. "Don't forget," she said. "You tell Armando no if he tries to bother you. You just had a baby. You tell him Alfonsina says he can't bother you."

"He won't listen," the mother said.

"Ah," said Alfonsina. "If it was Donna Vecchio said it, he would listen. They all listen to Donna Vecchio. She makes it fall off with her magic when they don't listen. You should have called Donna Vecchio for your baby."

Alfonsina opened the door. She was already in the hall when the mother touched her arm. The mother pointed to the package wrapped in newspaper.

"You swear to me, Alfonsina," she said.

"Yes, yes, I swear. Rest now or the milk won't come. And then where will you be? You and your mixed-up baby?"

When Alfonsina had gone, the mother picked up the baby. The baby was bound in strips of bedsheet, beginning under the arms and pulled tightly to the toes, where Alfonsina had tied a knot.

"You have to do this," she had told the mother, "to make the legs grow straight."

But now the mother unwrapped the baby and let her legs kick free. She sat in the chair by the window that looked out into the yard and the lines of laundry. She undid her dress. She wasn't worried about the milk. With the other baby, the one that couldn't swallow, there had been so much milk that when the baby died, no one could make the milk go away, until Donna Vecchio had come with her powers of *fattura* and a paste of olive oil and parsley. Donna Vecchio would be angry that she wasn't called for this baby.

The mother tried not to be afraid. This was America. She tried not to be afraid of Donna Vecchio. She tried not to be afraid of Armando.

Armando, who had come to her brother's house in Brooklyn one day to ask for her.

"Yes," her brother's wife had said.

"Who is he?" her brother had asked his wife that night when she told him.

"He's *Genovese*," his wife had said.

"But what does he do?" her brother had asked.

"He's *Genovese*, I told you," the wife had said. "What are you worried about? The *Genovese* always make a dollar. The undertaker, the butcher, all *Genovese*."

"She's a child," her brother said.

"She's old enough."

Armando had come and taken her from her brother's house with the front yard in Brooklyn and brought her here to the building across from the horse stables. She had carried her own things.

Once she had gone to her brother, and her brother had said that he would kill Armando with a knife.

But this was America.

Could she see her brother in jail because of Armando? She had come back alone to the building across from the horse stables.

The mother sat in the chair by the window with her baby. She heard the men coming home from work and the children called in from the street. She heard them on the stairs and smelled the cooking from their mothers' open doors.

Outside the window the laundry had disappeared. Empty clotheslines crisscrossed the yard. The mother looked out the window to where her girl would go, not to hang laundry, she was determined, and she waited for Armando.

Armando, who would come home and shout that there was no coal, that there was no food. He would try to bother her or he would be too drunk. He would not remember about the baby. She would not tell him.

If the shouting got too loud, if Armando banged too hard and too long on the door and the women got frightened, they would call the police. The police would come to the building across from the horse stables. They had come before, because this was America.

The men would not interfere. Behind the door was Armando's house. It would be the women who would call the police, and the police would come and make her open the door. They would make her let Armando into his house.

The men would nod. It was Armando's house. The women would stand in the hall with their heads covered. Some things do not change.

In the morning the baby cried. The mother made a fire in the stove. She ate bread and drank coffee and sat in the chair by the window with her baby.

A policeman came. He asked the mother to come with him. She wrapped the baby, covered her shoulders, and followed him to where they showed her Armando, his face battered and bloodless.

"An accident," the policeman said, "a fight. We don't know yet. Do you know anything?" he asked.

"I don't know anything," she told him.

"We'll find out," he said.

She knew they wouldn't.

When she came home, the women were waiting for her. They were waiting on the stoops and they were waiting by their open doors.

"Armando is dead," she told them.

Alfonsina came. She called out to the Virgin and Santa Rosalina. "I heard," she said. "I just heard about Armando." She took a package wrapped in newspaper from under her skirts.

"I brought it back," she said. "We can do it now. We can flush it down the toilet now. You don't need no more trouble."

"Give it to me," the mother said.

Alfonsina crossed herself. She swore she would say nothing, and she left the mother and the baby and the package wrapped in newspaper that she had carried under her skirts.

Armando came into the house that night in the undertaker's box. He lay on the white satin inside the box in the black suit he was married in. The people came and gave the mother money folded inside envelopes. The women whispered and shook their heads. She was young to have no husband. Why didn't she cry?

The men standing in the corners talked of other things. Some of them watched her too closely. She was young, they thought. She would get lonely. Maybe, when some time had passed . . .

The paid mourners in black shawls moaned over Armando's body. They moved back and forth over him, shaking water blessed by the priest from their fingers. The water made damp spots on Armando's black wedding suit.

Donna Vecchio came. When Donna Vecchio came, everything stopped. Her hair was done in marcelled waves. Her hairdresser lived in her house. Donna Vecchio had large breasts and short, bent legs. The envelope she gave the mother smelled of lavender.

"I'm sorry for your trouble," Donna Vecchio said. "And how is the baby?"

"Do you want to see her?" the mother said.

"The baby isn't mine," Donna Vecchio said. "You didn't call me for this baby. She isn't one of mine."

"But she is," the mother said. "I am giving her your name, Carolina. I am asking you to baptize her, to be her *gummara*."

Donna Vecchio smiled and held out her hand for a kiss.

• • •

The rows of borrowed chairs were empty. The mother sat alone. She would sit all night to watch for Armando's spirit. When the spirit of the dead leaves, it looks for a sleeping body to enter. It enters through the mouth.

The mother wouldn't sleep, but would sit all night with Armando, with the sound of the ice melting into the pan underneath his coffin. She would not let the baby sleep.

Underneath Armando's body was a block of ice, and underneath Armando's head, underneath the white satin pillow, was the package wrapped in newspaper.

And tomorrow they would bury Armando. They would put him in the ground with the afterbirth of the baby, in a hole so deep the dogs don't find it.

SISTER-IN-LAW

Get in the car.

I started to turn but there was a gun in my back or something pretending to be a gun. I faced forward. The voice was familiar, a woman's voice, a cigarette voice. Philip Morris unfiltered. I think that's the only way Philip Morris comes. Smoking them was a grand statement, too big for me, but if I was right about the voice then we'd shared a few together, she and I.

Angela?

Just get in the car. On your left.

She leaned over and opened the door and moved back. I got in. Her husband, Joey, was driving. He was a small guy and it was a big car. He looked like he was sitting in a hole. It was Buddy's car, a white Cadillac convertible with rocket fins and red leather interior, but the top was up, black and ominous.

Joey? I said.

Joey stared straight ahead, didn't even check me out in the rearview mirror. I was disappointed. I thought Joey liked me, but then I was always thinking people liked me when they really didn't give a shit. I felt better that I was in the backseat with Angela and not in the front with Joey. I knew about the piano wire around the neck, though this was no movie.

I actually felt bad. Until just now, Angela had treated me like family.

We were in the Village, on Barrow Street. I was on my way to meet Buddy at the restaurant he managed, next to the gay club he used to own, before the feds subpoenaed him to testify. He said that was when he learned to sweat and gave up red silk lining in his custom-made suits. Maybe saying the club he used to run is a better way to put it. Only one group of people owned clubs in Greenwich Village, but it was undisclosed ownership. The State Liquor Authority kept close tabs on who got a liquor license and who didn't.

Why did I know all this? I shouldn't have. My criminal involvement began and ended with my father's Prohibition bootlegging days and his stint as a bookkeeper for Tony Bender in the '30s. Good with numbers and honest, my father wasn't looking for power and glory, just enough money to start a legitimate business and buy a house. So how did I end up in a white Cadillac with rocket fins and this crazy bitch who was about to become my sister-in-law holding a gun on me?

I asked Angela where we were going. It was a legitimate question, I thought, under the circumstances.

Does it matter? she said.

I shrugged and she pulled my hair.

Staten Island? I said.

Bingo. She laughed.

My brother bragged how you were a college girl, Angela said. Me, I always thought you didn't have the brains God gave you. Angela really laughed when she said this. Hard to believe we grew up on the same street, she said to me.

I could have mentioned that she was a full ten years older than I was and her father wore overalls to work and gambled his paycheck before he got home Fridays, but her mouth was up close to my ear, her perfume was up my nose, and she was poking that gun hard in my ribs.

I met Buddy in Manhattan but he told me he lived out on Staten Island. Right away I knew something was up. He'd grown up in the Village. Staten Island? For me, Staten Island was Middlin' Beach and my mother's stories about the rented summer bungalow thirteen blocks from the ocean her first married summer when she was twenty and had a newborn baby (not me). My father took the ferry out every weekend. My mother thought she'd died and went to heaven. Her eight brothers and sisters thought so too, and came out every chance they got. No screens, no plumbing. I don't remember the amusement park or my cousins making human pyramids on the beach for the camera but there was an old 16 mm movie of me in white underpants licking the block of ice that sat on the porch.

What I'm saying is that, for me, Staten Island didn't conjure images of the high life. It was somewhere you went to if you were on the lam, it seemed that far away; where you went when you owed the wrong people money, the guys with the broken noses, Buddy called them, or when you couldn't go back to the neighborhood, like Angela, who needed a place to keep her husband straight after he got out of prison. Her mother watched the kids and the old man's insurance policy, which paid double after he was crushed between the ship and the pier, paid for the house on Florence Street that was a primo fixer-upper. Buddy said that when he came back from California after his marriage broke up, they were sitting on orange crates with candles stuck in those wine bottles with the straw bottoms.

We drove through the Midtown Tunnel and onto the BQE and I could see the Verrazano—for my money, the best thing about Staten Island. We turned left off the bridge and drove down what always felt to me like a country lane. The houses were old, the colors of old houses, green and brown. They had patches of grass in the front. Hylan Boulevard curved and looped before it straightened out and you hit the traffic and the local guidos in muscle cars with music blasting, small strip malls with the same three or four stores, Chinese restaurants that would mix won ton and egg drop soup in one bowl, sandwich shops called Angelo's and Gino's with an overstuffed sub painted in primary colors on the plate glass window, bridal shops, catering halls, restaurants named Petruzzi's with lattice and cognac-colored windows and endless parking. The Staten Islanders loved outdoor parking. They loved parking lots better than garages because in a parking lot everyone could admire your good-looking, expensive car, and you could too.

Hylan Boulevard flooded in a sudden rain; it flooded bad. The semi-detached condos that had been built on the graveyard of grand old houses flooded too, and the cars parked to the sides of the front doors were moved to higher ground with the first sprinkle.

Angela?

Shut up, she said.

I turned my head and she rammed the gun in my side.

Don't look at me.

Why? Because I might recognize you?

Funny. You think you're so funny. Watch me laugh. You know, smarty-pants, you should have just stayed where you belonged and away from Buddy. So now just shut your big mouth.

Someone should have warned me when I met Buddy that his family was crazy, but who knew they were this crazy? And let me tell you, when I met Buddy I wasn't planning on anything long-term. All I wanted was a good time. And Buddy was a lot of fun. He knew everybody and had all kinds of connections.

We went to after-hours bars and gambling parlors, clubs with private shows in back. We walked past velvet ropes and got the best seats; drinks arrived at the table compliments of the house. There were bear hugs and cheek kisses.

But honestly, did I need a guy who was broke and living with his mother, his two kids, his sister, and a brother-in-law who had five-to-ten in Dannemora under his belt? Living on Staten Island no less? Buddy was pretty quiet about the Staten Island piece and hinted that it wasn't so bad and maybe we could live out there after we got married. He was awful grateful to Angela for taking him in when the ex-wife grabbed the stash, dumped the kids, and went AWOL with a South American disco dancer named Chico.

We made the turn off the boulevard and onto Florence Street. I was starting to think Angela was really stupid. She kidnaps me at gunpoint and brings me to her house?

When Joey pulled into the driveway, I could see the television flickering with the kids planted in front of it. Angela and Joey had four kids of their own and they all watched television together and made popcorn on Saturday nights. The kind in the aluminum pan that you hold over the stove and the top blows up like a balloon.

Joey, I said, did you ever shoot anyone?

I thought I told you to shut up, Angela said, which made me open my eyes and look at her.

She was digging in her huge black alligator satchel (which for sure had "fallen off a truck," but who am I to talk?). Before she'd turned nasty, Angela would throw things my way when they came in pairs. Shit, I was wearing an 18-karat gold Rolex that had actually been special order, serial number and everything, from some guy who worked in the factory and swiped a few selectively every month. I was one to talk. Thinking about my watch made me look down at my wrist which Angela was trying to duct-tape to my other wrist. We both zeroed in on the watch at the same time and Angela ripped it off my arm.

Last year, she said, this would have been mine. Buddy would have bought it for me, so I'll just take it now.

I saw this as an opportunity and gave her an elbow to the lip and a slap on the side of her head, right on her ear. I had nothing to lose. I had read about serial killers. Once they get you tied up, you're done for. If only . . . Angela pulled back and punched me so hard that if I'd been a cartoon, the whole strip would have been nothing but stars.

When I opened my eyes again, Angela had taped my wrists together and tied me up. The rope was around my neck and connected to my duct-taped wrists, kind of a semi-hog-tie. A disgusting concept. I was hating Angela, not to mention Joey who was waving what I noticed was a very beautiful Beretta in my face. I recognized it as Buddy's gun. It was a pocket pistol— used, unfortunately. Buddy was going to give it to me—for protection, he said when he showed it to me. The only reason I didn't have it was that Buddy was waiting for a holster. Buddy liked everything just so.

Angela, I said, this is really stupid. What's going on? What do you want? For Chrissakes, I'm marrying your brother in six weeks. Take this shit off me!

She looked at her watch—I mean, my watch that seemed now to be hers. We've got a lot of time, she said to Joey. Buddy doesn't get home for hours.

There she was right. Buddy had two jobs, one at a restaurant and the other at a mob-owned nightclub somewhere in the Seventies in Manhattan where the boss had signed a half-dead Judy Garland while she was nodding off on pills. I was supposed to meet him at the restaurant for dinner but he didn't get off for the night until 4:00 A.M., which was hours and hours away.

Can I put down this goddamn gun, Angela? Joey said. And can we get moving? Would you quit yapping?

OK, OK. I thought you were ready. You mixed the cement, no?

It's not just the cement. I gotta move the rocks. They gotta fit. I want it to look nice.

I could feel the blood in the back of my throat; she must have broken my nose, the crazy bitch. I imagined the mouse starting under my eye.

You know we're in Great Kills, she said to me. Great Kills, get it? You're gonna be great killed. Angela thought this was hilarious.

I wasn't feeling so cocky right about then, I have to admit. I thought I was better than Angela. I mean, comparing us was like apples and pears, but if you want to know the truth, while I appreciated her finer qualities, ultimately I did feel she was a creature below.

Angela, talk to me. Let's figure this thing out, I said.

It's easy, she said. You're a college girl; you figure it out. But let me give you a hint. Buddy's got everything here. We take care of each other. We're family. He needs you like he needs a hole in the head. What's he got to go to Manhattan for? You wanna take the kids away from me? I love those kids. They call me Mama. They hug me so tight sometimes I can't breathe.

We can work something out, I told her. Maybe Buddy and I could live here. Maybe find a house nearby . . .

Buddy had hinted at this very plan and I had kiboshed it unequivocally. I'd lived in Rome and Paris and Bombay. I was going to live in Staten Island next to his sister?

You're full of shit, Angela said. Buddy told me he asked you and you said no.

I didn't. I never said no.

Buddy's a liar?

No, he just doesn't listen. You know, Angela, how he doesn't listen. Think about it. It could be great, all of us together.

She looked at me. I sensed that Joey was feeling bad for me. His hand wasn't shaking so much anymore. I willed him to put down the gun but he didn't. He just wasn't gripping it so tight that his hand shook.

Angela smiled. She was a beautiful girl. Black hair, skin like pearls dipped in milk. The first time I met her, she had on a one-shoulder dress and I swear I wanted to put my tongue against her skin and lick, it was that luscious.

I fell for that once, Angela said, with that other rat bastard. We were like sisters. Then look what I had to do. She took everything, but at least we got the kids. Joey and I took care of her, didn't we, Joey? But just my luck, we get rid of one son-of-a-bitch and Buddy finds another. He's a real pain in my ass sometimes, my brother.

Angela, be honest, Buddy's only here with you because—

Because what?

She didn't look so beautiful right now. I shut my mouth.

Because he had nowhere else to go, I wanted to say.

Buddy's mother always said she was sorry she gave up the tenement apartment on Spring Street. She didn't call it a tenement, though. She called it her "nice apartment." From Buddy I knew it was three rooms in the back, facing the alley, tub in the kitchen, and everyone waiting in the hallway when one of them took a bath on Saturdays. Tenements weren't Buddy's style and neither was Florence Street, from what I could see. There were more trees on Spring Street.

Joey had been "fixing up" the house on Florence Street ever since he'd gotten out. Joey was handy, he had what they called "hands of gold," which he seemed to use for ripping things out and never putting them back in, the bathroom on the second floor, for instance. We're getting a new bathroom, Angela had told me, but they'd been using the one in the basement for three years while Joey moved on to other projects, such as busting up the stairs so everyone had to walk up on a wooden ramp like the cart horses in the stable on Thompson Street.

And then there was Joey's wall. The first time Buddy took me to Florence Street, Joey was in the front yard mixing cement. There were piles of boulders, different sizes, and Joey was using them to build a wall. The kids were carrying over the smaller ones and Joey was fitting them on top of one another and side by side and cementing them in place. The wall belonged on an English country estate. The wall belonged on meadows and hills and dales. The wall was beautiful and ridiculous. The house was small and ugly and sat on a small and ugly lot, and then all around it, not more than ten feet out, was this magnificent stone wall that each time I visited got higher and higher, until it was starting to look like a rampart. Buddy laughed about it. He called it Joey's therapy. But I have to be honest, it gave me the creeps.

I'm tired of talking, Angela said to me. Get out of the car.

No, no. Leave her in the car until I'm ready, Joey said.

We can't leave her in the car. We'll put her in the basement while you set things up.

The basement? Did you ever carry dead weight up stairs? Joey said. I'm no Hercules and for sure, she ain't no lightweight.

I let the insult pass. I'm always surprised when people say mean things about me. As I said, I was always thinking people liked me when they really didn't give a shit. But all that aside, what the hell were they talking about?

I pulled at my wrists, but when I did, the rope tightened around my neck. I was afraid I would pee myself. I thought I'd bring up using the bathroom but I wanted to wait for the right time. Maybe I could get away then, make a noise, maybe I had a chance. The kids would hear, the old lady—deaf as she was— the dog, the neighbors not twenty feet away, someone.

Angela smiled. She can walk, she said. She can walk up the basement stairs. It'll be dark.

You're kidding me, Joey said.

I always believed in you, Joey. Even with that crazy wall. I always believed in you. That's why I stuck, through thick and thin.

I have to go to the bathroom, I said.

You wanna take her? Joey said.

Let her piss herself, Angela told him. She looked me straight in the face. Whatta we care?

Can you guess the rest? Joey put the gun to my temple. Angela duct-taped my mouth. She checked the rope around my wrists and my neck. She pulled me out of the car and down the basement steps. Joey wanted to put out a mat so I could lie down. Angela said no. I'd piss on it, remember I had asked to go to the bathroom? And then she'd have to throw it out and Clorox the place. She'll be lying down forever, Angela said. Just like the other one.

In the end, they put some blankets on the floor and pushed me down. I could smell dog on the wool but I was glad just to lie there and close my eyes. I heard them leave. I watched the light go away as the sun went down. I heard the scrape of the trowel. I heard one of Buddy's kids call out to Joey, asking him why he was working on the wall, it was nighttime. I think I slept. And then they were pulling me up. Angela and Joey. And walking me up the stairs.

There was no moon. I wondered what Buddy would think—if he would think that, like his first wife, I had just up and disappeared. Gotten cold feet? Left him at the altar? And the kids . . . would they feel abandoned again? Miss me? I noticed when I got close to the wall how wide it was, wide enough to lie down on. The wall was different heights in different parts. I wondered how high it would go in the end. I realized I would never know.

Angela took my arm and walked me to a place where the wall was low, maybe four feet, and she made me lie down. I felt the stones that jutted through the layer of cement hard against my back, my shoulders, my head, and then she picked up a boulder, so big that it blocked my vision. It would have blocked out the moon if there had been one in the sky, and she brought it down with all her strength.

Buddy came home early the next morning. When he woke up, he took his coffee into the yard where Joey was working on the wall. The kids were rolling stones. They were still in their pajamas.

It's really coming along, Buddy said. This wall is going to be here after we're all dead, Joey. It's like the goddamn Colosseum.

The phone rang and someone inside picked it up. Is that for me? Buddy shouted.

You expecting a call? Joey said.

I thought it might be Annemarie. She never showed up last night.

She ever done that before?

No, Buddy said. Never.

MOTHER LOVE

Piero would ride in a basket that his mother had set upon her head. She would cover him with a white cloth and go walking in the streets of the city.

From the basket he would put out his hand and snatch off the hats of the men passing by. The men would look around and they would see a woman with a basket on her head, a basket covered with a white cloth.

These were his beginnings.

Piero and his mother were everything in the world to each other. The father had gone long ago. "America ate him up," the mother said when Piero asked. "But you are my little man, and I don't need any other."

When she said this, she would wet her fingers in her mouth and smooth down his hair. His hair was thick and black like his father's before he went to America.

Piero would stand very close to his mother when she did this. He marveled that he could feel the heat of her through all the skirts she wore, one over the other like the gypsy women at the edge of the city.

The gypsy women would steal him, his mother said, if he weren't careful. They would cover him with their skirts and take him away. No one would know where, his mother told him. Piero secretly wanted to go close to them, to be caught under their skirts. He wanted to know if they had heat like his mother but he was too afraid.

On Saturdays Piero and his mother would go to the market to sell the hats. He would set up the table for his mother and step back when he was finished. And then he would think about slipping under her skirts. He wanted to sit with the silk of her underskirt in his fingers while she bargained for the price of the hats. He liked the darkness under her skirts. He closed his eyes and remembered the smell of her. It was their secret.

"Go away now," she would shout at him when he came close, loud enough to make the shutters open. She would sit on the small stool she had carried from home and spread her skirts around her. "A boy must not stay too near his mother," she told him in a whisper. "Remember Anzio? Anzio who stayed near his mother? Remember Anzio?"

"Was that God? Did God do that to Anzio?" Piero asked, terrified.

"The witches did that," the mother said, "the witches here in the *rione*. They don't like a boy who stays near his mother. They're jealous."

Piero was afraid when he though of Anzio. His mother's words made him run away and he would not come back until it was time to take down her table and carry it home.

But when they came to the small room where they lived together, Piero's mother would close the curtains on the window that looked over the street and she would call him to her, even before she made their meal.

Everyone in this city stayed where they were born. Everyone stayed in their *rione* and married in their *rione* and died there. But not Piero's father. He went outside to marry. His bride was a stranger in the *rione* and she had red hair. He married outside the *rione* which is not what young men should do.

"So many beauties here," the gossips said. "Why did he go outside?"

Piero's mother called them witches. When Piero was born she hung *cornetti* of coral and silver and even a tiny one made of gold over his cradle. He was such a beautiful and strong baby boy, Piero's mother said, that they were powerless to harm him and so they used their evil magic on his father and his father went away.

This is what Piero's mother told him.

"Won't he come back? Don't you think he'll come back?" Piero wanted to know.

"No," his mother said.

"Why? Why won't he come back to us?"

"The witches," his mother said. "There was black rain when he left. He is never coming back."

"Aren't you sad? Don't you cry for him to come back?" Piero asked her.

The mother kissed the top of his head where the black hair parted.

"Don't I have you?" she said. "How can I be sad?"

Piero would put his head in her lap and close his eyes when she said this. He didn't care about his father or the witches who worried her. He would close his eyes and touch her there. He would sleep in her heat and her smell.

Piero grew bigger and his mother older. The shine was gone from her hair that was red like no one else's in the *rione*. When Piero grew too big for the basket she used it to carry washing.

Piero moved through the streets in far parts of the city by himself now, and took the things they needed. Sometimes he went to the edge of the city to watch the gypsies who could no longer steal him away under their skirts. He was a grown boy.

The mother prayed to keep Piero hers. She put blessed palm under his mattress and made promises to her saint. But the summer that Piero was big enough, he got himself a girl. The girl was of the *rione*, from the family that mended umbrellas, and she was small and soft like the bunnies Piero kept at Easter. The girl would take him into the alleys and lift up her skirts for him. Piero loved her smell.

The mother prayed to her saint. She explained that all she had ever had was Piero and her red hair. She asked the saint to make Piero like Anzio even though that was a terrible thing for a mother to ask. She asked for a sign but the saint was silent while Piero's girl whispered in his ear. She pulled up her skirts. "We should marry," she said.

"My mother . . . ," Piero said.

"Your mother is a witch. She has that red hair," the girl said.

Piero got angry. He pinched the soft flesh on the inside of the girl's arm. "I am my mother's son," he told her.

"You are your father's son," the girl said. "Your hair is black. You belong in the *rione*. Your mother is from outside."

"She only has me," Piero said.

"She only wants you," the girl told him. "She made the black rain so your father would leave and never come back."

Piero stepped away.

"Your mother is a witch and you are under her spell."

This is what the girl told Piero.

On Piero's wedding day, the mother did not touch her son. She could see in his eyes that he did not want her to touch him. The mother embraced the bride and smiled at Piero. She put her hand slowly through her red hair and made Piero afraid.

When Piero came out of the house the morning after his wedding night, his mother was there. The empty basket was set upon her head.

"I am here to hang the sheet," she said. "It's my right as your mother. The *rione* is waiting to see the blood on the sheet."

"There isn't any blood," Piero said.

"All virgins have blood," she told him.

His mother reached out to touch him but he moved away. He didn't want to be so near her. He remembered Anzio.

"Don't worry," Piero's mother said to him.

Piero left her and walked to the coffee bar. He stood with the men who teased him about his wedding night. They serenaded him with bawdy songs.

The women leaned out of the shadows, their arms folded across the windowsills. They were waiting to see the sheet, to see the blood.

They all watched when Piero's mother came out of the house with the basket on her head. They watched as she hung out the bloodied sheet.

The men squinted their eyes in the morning sun. Piero's mother moved along the clothesline. She held the clothespins in her mouth. The blood from the sheet dripped onto the paving stones.

"So much blood," the women in the windows said. "We've never seen so much blood."

The mother fastened the last clothespin to the edge of the sheet. The blood ran in little rivers between the blocks of stone. The mother turned and smiled at Piero and put her hand through her red hair.

FISH HEADS

The hostel was dreary. Jakarta felt polluted, crowded and dirty after the island paradise of Bali, where we had rented a room in a family compound and discovered fruits worthy of fairy tales: mangoes, mangosteens, jackfruit, papaya, and pale yellow pineapples cut into wedges. An enterprising young woman named Jenik had gotten herself a blender and access to electricity and, at a stand on the dirt road to Kuta Beach in 1968, smoothies came to town. Jenik also figured out pancakes and French toast and would make omelettes with dirty blue-gray mushrooms. Her eggs, your mushrooms. Magic! But for how long can you watch the sunset and dance with the Barong? We had left home for adventure, to tip over the edge of comfort and familiarity, and Bali was only the first stop. We didn't have much of a plan, but we knew we were moving and had all the time in the world.

In Sydney we'd bought a series of tickets that would take us through Java and Sumatra to Singapore. We had bus tickets, ferry tickets, and chits that would get us lifts on trucks in Sumatra. We had small bags and bellies full of nasi goreng and chicken satay. We'd had a Christmas feast at a Chinese restaurant in Denpasar with turtle soup and a collection of roasted and lacquered birds that, if they had still had their feathers, would have flown away. We'd roasted goats on spits over wood fires on the beach and piglets in pits of charcoal. We were loving Indonesia. The dreary hostel and grimy city would be left behind as soon as we'd washed our clothes and changed some money.

The night before we were to leave Jakarta, a man came to the hostel dormitory. I don't remember if we thought it was odd that he was there, or how the conversation started, but he made us an offer that we thought we couldn't, and shouldn't, refuse. He convinced us that the overland trek to Singapore was a terrible undertaking. Unreliable transport, he said. Impenetrable jungle. Mosquitoes. Nowhere even remotely decent to eat or sleep. And it would take weeks. And it was the rainy season. What were we thinking? There were six of us. We looked at each other. Of course, our new friend had the solution. A ship to Singapore. Ocean breezes, deck chairs, all meals included for the seven-day journey. I personally loved ships, loved being at sea, had sweet memories of crossing the Atlantic on the Italian line, coming to Australia on a freighter. Someone poked me. What would it cost? Important point. It sounded like a big-ticket item. We were backpackers, remember? someone said. One new friend said not to worry. He would make it happen for us. He'd take our existing tickets plus a few extra rupiah. A bargain, he said.

We parted with our tickets and rupiah and the next morning we were at the dock, along with, it seemed, a thousand others—despite the appearance that the ship had no accommodations for passengers. It was outfitted for cargo, clearly. Pandemonium reigned. We made a quick decision to follow the crowd. We were the only foreigners but we were used to that, so we climbed the gangplank and got on board. Families were claiming spots, laying down mats. Space was tight because of the cargo, which appeared to be garbage, piled up high in the bow. There was also no way we were changing our minds and getting back off. The crowd was only moving one way. We spread out our sleeping bags and sat down on the deck. I had a flashback to summers in Coney Island, with beach blankets laid end to end held down by shoes and radios. The ship pulled out. Our fellow passengers started getting sick almost immediately. I closed my eyes and leaned against my backpack. Believe it or not, I was hungry.

I took good food for granted. I grew up a first-generation Italian American. We weren't big on ambience (I don't think I saw a milk pitcher until I was of legal age) but we knew about food. Lamb at Easter, the rib chops as tiny as a baby's fist, the lamb's head, capozelle, split and roasted with parsley, garlic and parmigiano; minestrone soup with five kinds of fresh beans and gobs of pesto stirred in; veal shoulder stuffed with egg and bread and oregano. When I started traveling, I didn't know much about the world or what there was to see, but I was open to what there was to eat. Camembert in France, ham sandwiches with butter (butter? hmmm), pork-liver pâté. In Italy, puntarella and buffalo mozzarella, sautéed rabbit, fresh figs. Yogurt and honey in Greece and feta with tomatoes and cucumbers; profiteroles, zaatar bread, King of Persia pistachios, roasted corn, duck eggs swallowed raw in a tea glass on the road overland to India.

A gong sounded. People started to stir, then slowly stampede. A line formed that snaked the length of the ship. I didn't see any food. I didn't smell any food, but a gong and what could pass as a queue facing in one direction was enough for me. I imagined rice and vegetables with a fried egg on top, soup with scallions and cabbage and pillows of tofu, maybe a shred of pork or chicken. I hadn't eaten since early morning. The line moved but I was too far away to see anything. I smiled at the babies; pushed with the best of them. I was very hungry and nearing my turn.

And soon, there in front of me were the servers, ladling food onto tin plates from two huge oil drums. I was pushed from behind, handed a tin plate, and pushed again.

I looked down. A ball of rice and two silvery fish heads. Maybe there were three. Fish heads? I liked the look of a whole fish on a plate as well as anyone: braised with ginger, or roasted with fennel. I even liked the way a whole fish looked after it was eaten. A charming head and tail and a beautiful skeleton of bones.

The rice was gummy, the fish heads were small, stuck in the rice, eyes staring. I didn't know what to do with them except look for a cat! My companions, English and Australian, gave back their plates and left the line empty-handed. They hadn't liked the Christmas turtle soup or the lacquered goose poised in flight. They pooled their money with a plan to bribe the crew. I decided not to give up. I was very hungry. I took my tin plate and went back to my place on the deck. I formed some rice into a ball with my fingers and shoveled it into my mouth with my thumb. The fish heads looked at me. I picked one up and studied it. I poked at it with my fingers and found a small round of sweet white flesh at the cheek. And more to eat in the furrow at the top of the head, and above the eyes, at the forehead (if fish have a forehead). I broke it apart and sucked the bones. I ignored the eyes and gelatinous bits (personally, aspic gives me shivers) and I started on the second head. I finished the rice. I rinsed my fingers and my plate. My travel friends, meanwhile, had managed to score a pineapple and a bag of mandarins for a small fortune. They set about rationing like shipwrecked sailors. I accepted a mandarin section.

I have always liked fruit after a meal. I unzipped my sleeping bag and lay down on the deck. I dreamt of fish heads.

The next day lunch was fish heads and rice and dinner was fish heads and rice. Twice a day, every day, for seven days, I ate fish heads. I found more tasty bits. I found the joy in fish heads. I smiled at the babies. I breathed in the sea air.

The ship ultimately left us, not in Singapore, but on a tiny island off Malaysia that had never seen a tourist, where the police were kind enough to put us up in a jail cell for the night, and for another small fortune, we hired a boat to take us to Singapore. We went straight to Maxwell Road to eat amazing dishes at the open-air market: Hokkein mee (fried prawn noodles), Hainanese chicken rice, chili crab. I didn't miss the fish heads. But I've never forgotten them.

There was an old Italian man in my neighborhood who had served time in Alcatraz. In "the hole," he said, they fed him bread and water. "I'd put the bread aside," he told me, "and after two days it tasted like cake . . ." In Indonesia, I learned what he meant.

MARGUERITE

"You'll be cut to pieces before you're fifty miles across the
Border," I said. "You have to travel through Afghanistan to
get to that country. It's one mass of mountains and peaks
and glaciers, and no Englishman has been through it."
—Rudyard Kipling, *The Man Who Would Be King*

The first time I met Marguerite she was wearing bedsheets. She had dyed them colors, pinks and purples, and sewn
them into pajamas. She wore many sets, one on top of the
other, and told me she would shed them, one by one, as the
weather got warmer, until in Goa she would be naked. Her
hair was orange from henna and her eyes half shut from opium
but I didn't understand that then.

We were in Istanbul, sleeping at the Gülhane, drinking tea
at the Pudding Shop in Sultanahmet. Marguerite was alone but
I was with Oliver who, as I saw it, had rescued me from a life
measured in church bells and cheap cigarettes. I had seduced
him on the floor of the dining room where we had set our
sleeping bags side by side in the home of mutual friends when
I heard he was on his way to India. I had been calculating. Men
were easy to seduce, unless you loved them. It was always easier
not to love them. God knows, they could be cruel.

Even Oliver, fragile as a flower, would in the end be heartless. Oliver, brilliant and beautiful, with his clipped overwrought language ripened at Cambridge, *The Golden Bough* in his rucksack. Where I come from, a man is said to be beautiful when he looks like a girl. Handsome was something else. Handsome made the heart beat. Beauty made you sigh. You wanted to reach out and touch its cheek.

Oliver was beautiful, with the perfect face of a fairy-tale prince. He wore his hair in a pageboy and I called him Prince Valiant but not to his beautiful face. I was living an interior life. Where I come from, men have rough ways and big noses and are always touching their crotches.

I was smug when we left the next morning, hand in hand. We took the train to Istanbul. Even Oliver, who counted the pennies in his palm, had to let go of hitchhiking somewhere in the south of Yugoslavia.

THE ISTANBUL TRAIN STATION
NOVEMBER 15, 1969
5:00 A.M.

When the train pulled into the station I saw him standing there and at that moment I remembered the warnings I had been given as a girl about the *colpo di fulmine*, when your heart is split open as though by lightning. A dangerous event. How can you protect yourself when your heart is split in two?

He was all I could see. Black curls, black eyes, hands in pockets, alone, grinning. A mythological creature, a satyr.

I think of him standing on the tracks in front of the train. How could he have been? I was delusional, too long alone on the road with the beautiful, brilliant, parsimonious Oliver. I closed my eyes. The train moved further into the station and he was gone.

Oliver went to rent us dormitory beds and I made my way down to the Pudding Shop. The Pudding Shop. Germans, Dutch, French, English back from the East, draped in satin and silk and beads, languorous, with kohled eyes, and, yes, beautiful.

And there was Marguerite, in her bedsheets, carefully rolling an English joint. "I'm Dutch," she said, between licking the many papers it took to make a real English joint. She had a chipped front tooth and slurred the words, her accent heavy. "My English is not so good."

"Your English is great," I said.

"I go to India," she said.

"Me, too," I told her.

"We go together. *Ja*, why not?" she said. She ran her tongue the length of the joint to seal it and tore a piece of cardboard from a package of Murad cigarettes to make a filter. The joint was conical and when she lit it, the tip burned red in a circle the size of a nickel. "*Ja*, you come with us. We go tomorrow. We take the train." She handed me the joint.

"I'm with someone," I said. "An Englishman."

"You bring him. Good. He comes too." She closed her eyes and seemed to sleep.

Oliver came in and sat down. He put another sugar cube in my tea glass and drank what was left. "This is Marguerite," I said. "She's going to India on the train tomorrow and wants us to go with her." Oliver blinked. I handed him the joint. Marguerite's eyes fluttered open.

"She's a junkie," he said. "We're not going anywhere with her. And besides, we are stopping at Ankara. There are things I want to see there."

Marguerite looked at Oliver and she shrugged. I was sad and a little bit pissed. I moved closer to her on the bench until she was leaning against me. I had fallen a little bit in love with her. I loved her more in the days that were to come. This was not the end by any means.

Oliver left and I ordered another tea and a rice pudding. "He is pretty," Marguerite said.

Oliver *was* pretty, I thought. I had a beautiful man. My old man was beautiful. Still, since that night on the dining room floor, we hadn't touched. It would be many weeks before he touched me again. And terrible things had to happen before he did. I will tell you but you will have to wait.

"But why do you go with him?" she asked me.

I looked at her. Until she asked, it had been obvious to me what I was doing with Oliver. I told her even as I told myself. "He's taking me to India," I said, and watched her eyelids close again.

I had been living in Italy with the spoiled only son of a rich Milanese family who did not use their influence when he was called up for compulsory military service. His father might have thought it would make him a man. And so I followed him to a dark mountain village where the children threw stones when I came to the square to shop. His mother had sent us off with a small cheese grater for parmigiano.

The dark village was most likely beautiful, the birthplace of popes, high in the Dolomites, but I have never loved mountains, I told Marguerite. What I did love was the preening *Alpini* of the elite Italian army unit, who came to the bars in their medieval velvet hats with long white plumes. My Milanese was not one of these.

Enter an invitation to Sorrento, enter Oliver, the piece of cake passing through Sorrento on his way to India, enter me, the seducer, looking for a way out.

"And your Italian lover?" The question startled me. I didn't think she was listening.

We passed through Belluno to get my things. I left Oliver in the bar with the plumed *Alpini*. I came into the house like a thief in the night although it was mid-afternoon. The plan was to gather up my things and disappear. I didn't consider a note. I can be a sneak.

But my Milanese also came like a thief in the night. He cursed me, and tore my photograph into small pieces and threw them in my face. I stood and took my medicine. I understood consequences. Where I come from, you pay for your sins. I left the cheese grater. I felt badly but I just wanted to go. I wanted to get away from the terrible curses.

So, is there a happy ending? Does the adventurer/seductress make her way to the East and find fulfillment? Hell, no. I blame the curses, which, eventually, hit their mark.

Marguerite started another joint and told me she had left Amsterdam alone. The dope was getting too expensive. She didn't like the cold. She kept getting pregnant. She had a fake passport in a man's name and sixty US dollars in traveler's checks that someone had given her. She was going to Goa. For Christmas. "Everyone," she said, waving her hand to indicate the room. "All. Goa for Christmas!"

The youth of Western Europe and America were on the move. I smoked with Marguerite until I thought I had gone blind, paid for her tea and found my way to the dormitory room in the Gülhane. I fell asleep on the narrow cot next to Oliver's wearing all my clothes. It was cold in Istanbul.

THE ISTANBUL TRAIN STATION
NOVEMBER 16, 1969
2:00 P.M.

We came to buy our tickets to Ankara, Oliver and I, according to his plan.

"Where are you going to, mate?"

I stood mute while my Istanbul train station satyr, my destiny, my destruction, spoke to Oliver. I looked over at Oliver and, at that moment, it seemed to me that his heart too had been struck. Oliver stared at Rick.

I was ignored by both of them. I stayed silent. I listened to Rick, his name was Rick, he said, from Yorkshire, tell Oliver that we couldn't stop in Ankara. We had to push on through Turkey. There was a group of them leaving that night. It was important to be in a group, Rick said. "The Turks, the women . . ." He pointed his chin at me. "You don't know what you're doing, mate, traveling with a bird."

And just like that, we were in the Grand Bazaar buying kilos of nuts and dried fruit. Rick bought cashews and apricots and figs. Oliver, pennies in his palm, stuck to peanuts and raisins.

Oliver, we would say where I come from, as I may have convinced you by now, didn't go for spit. Oliver wouldn't spend a wooden nickel. Oliver could squeeze a dollar until it cried. Oliver, we would say where I come from, was a cheap son-of-a-bitch. But Oliver was my ticket to ride.

THE ISTANBUL TRAIN STATION
NOVEMBER 16, 1969
8:00 P.M.

Rick saw us when we came into the station. He smiled, he waved. Oliver and I moved toward him. He stood in the center of a group, the one he insisted we go with to India.

And there, on the edge of the group, was Marguerite. She wore a purple blanket as a shawl, and underneath, the layers of pajamas that she had sewn from bedsheets. She had a small cloth bag hanging from around her neck. Inside, she told me, were her documents, and she showed me the passport of Lars Dekker, a young man with dark hair. I was so glad to see her, to be traveling with her, but I worried. She shrugged, newly high, and scratched her arms. "Pshew," she said. "No one tells the difference. A Dutch passport is a Dutch passport. The worst?" she said. "I go to the Dutch embassy and they send me home."

Rick herded us onto the train and we took over a compartment. There was a South African girl and two French boys, by their eyes and their energy, high on opium. For four days and nights, we huddled against each other, shoulder to shoulder, hip to hip. Turks rattled the door when they spied Marguerite's orange hair and Rick made her cover her head with the purple blanket which she was happy to do. The light hurt her eyes.

The French boys and Marguerite were sick, drug sick. They were coming down, crashing. Oliver, too, was sick, his stomach as delicate as his face. My satyr and I smoked joints and ate cashews and figs and apricots. He trailed me to the toilet to protect me from the Turks. He taught me how to roll a proper English joint.

HOW TO ROLL A PROPER ENGLISH JOINT

Start with a minimum of three papers.

Two side by side and one across the top so you have a T shape.

Lick the glue strips on the edge of the papers and put them together.

Flatten the paper on your leg and press with your forearm.

Cloth against cloth to keep the seal.

Slit open a cigarette and take out the tobacco.

Burn the hashish with a flame until it's soft.

Crumple it into the tobacco.

Mix well.

Spread the mix down the center of the rolling papers and shape into a cone.

Lick the seam.

Tear a strip of cardboard from a cigarette pack.

Roll it up like a ribbon and insert into the small end of the joint.

Light and smoke.

I wanted the train ride to go on forever, the gravy train, the train to glory, but we reached the end of the line, Erzurum, a pit of a town near the Iranian border where Marguerite was almost kidnapped by a shopkeeper when she went in to look at a necklace. Rick shook his head. "Birds," he said.

We crossed into Iran, Marguerite's passport stamped as easily as the rest, and got a bus to Tabriz where we all shared a dank, cold room. The French boys scored and nodded through the night with Marguerite curled against them. I slept in my clothes with my elegant floor-length woven wool coat buttoned to the neck. I had it custom-made in Milan when my life was different.

The next day we left for Teheran and the Amir Kabir Hotel, where we shared another dank, cold room with a stove we couldn't light because Rick said the fumes would kill us while we slept. Rick told us all what to do, leading us this way and that.

We were a motley crew at this point. The South African girl had hit the end of the road. No country further on would give her a visa and she decided to turn back. Oliver was consumed with dysentery while Marguerite and the French boys cooked a ball of opium and sat on their cots trying to pierce a vein with a blunt needle.

I had no will of my own. I was a bird in a cage, a dog on a leash. I watched the French boys with their opium ritual, the spoon, the flame, the black bubbling tar, the needle filling with blood, the bright red of it disappearing into the blackness of the opium. The way their bodies went limp. Only Marguerite suffered, the veins in her arms and legs collapsed and hidden. The French boys were trying to help, but they were so stoned.

I was fascinated but Rick was disgusted and pulled me away. We went into the street, he and I. It was Ramadan and we slid under the gates of a café shuttered to inches above the ground in deference to the holiday that forbade food and drink and sex from sunrise to sunset. By candlelight we ate rice as light as air and bread folded like newspaper. We drank sweet tea.

"Who are you?" Rick said. "What are you doing with this bloke? Are you together?"

What do you mean? I thought but didn't say. He's my boy-friend, I thought. He's my old man. Isn't he far out? Isn't he beautiful? He's taking me to India to live on the beach. He's taking me to Goa for Christmas.

Rick tore off a piece of bread. He looked at me, a devil, those black eyes, a mouthful of white, white teeth. "If you were my old lady," he said, "I can tell you we wouldn't be sleeping in a dormitory room." The scales fell from my eyes but he looked away.

Back at the hotel, Marguerite and the French boys were on the nod. Oliver was curled up in a corner. "Let's go," Rick said. "The bus to the border leaves in an hour." Oliver stood up. Marguerite moaned. The French boys held up their hands in defeat.

"Marguerite, Marguerite, get up, come on," I said. "We're leaving. We're going to India . . . to the sun, the beach."

"We see each other," she said to me.

"We can't leave them here like this," I said, but Rick scowled at me.

"Look at them," he said. "They have everything they need."

I couldn't imagine Marguerite would ever make it out of that room but I left. I followed Rick, Oliver trailing behind, and now we were three. And everyone knows that three's a crowd. But I was the center of the crowd and that's never a bad place to be, or so I thought. I had more than I had bargained for and I had no idea what would happen next.

We crossed the no-man's-land and spent the night at the Afghan border, me and my men. The border guards brought us hashish and I breathed easy. The night was cold, the sky filled with stars. Oliver slept. I rolled English joints and smoked them with Rick.

Back in Iran, under portraits of the Shah, we could have gone to jail for life. Smugglers from Afghanistan were executed if they were caught but the Afghans smuggled anyway, under the orders of their tribal chiefs. They crossed the border on horseback, fearless.

We had scored in a back alley of Teheran, the hashish seller in pajamas, having come out a window near a construction site. Rick the negotiator, Oliver the bystander, me, the woman, Adam's rib.

There were not so many women on the trail East, and of the ones alone, I remember only two: Marguerite, and a magnificent Swedish blonde I saw on Chicken Street in Kabul, wearing wolf fur, a miniskirt, and high black boots. I wanted to touch her to see if she were real. I never saw or heard of her again.

We arrived in Herat where the man at the hotel said we could wash. It had been seven days and nights and I peeled off my clothes, watched the fire he made to heat the water. I had two sets of clothes, the one I was wearing, the other clean and folded in my bag. Purple jeans and a purple wool sweater. I thought of Marguerite in her lavender bedsheets, her eyes closed, her foot bleeding where she had finally found a vein.

I washed my hair and stood combing it by the window. Rick said, "Let's go," and the three of us left. We got into a taxi. He slid in first and when I moved in beside him, his hand was under me. We rode through the streets, Rick's hand up between my legs, Oliver oblivious on my other side. Rick talked, laughed, directed the driver, as though his hand was not under me, moving between my legs. I squeezed my thighs together, guilty, longing. My fate was sealed.

That night as we lay on our cots, side by side, the three of us, I waited, eyes open in the dark, but there was nothing but breathing and the smell of the wood fire.

We continued, we three, long bus rides through the mountains and desert, through Kandahar, where Rick took us into the bazaar to buy a block of hashish. He had been here before. He knew his way around, he said, and we went into a stall, elevated above the street, and sat cross-legged on rugs and drank tea. I knew better than to speak.

"*Hunum?*" the men would ask. Rick would laugh and shake his head yes. Oliver would blink. Whose *hunum* was I, I wondered. I made myself stand still, an object of curiosity. I was covered and in the company of men so I was left alone. It was a relief to be relieved of explaining myself—No mother? No father? No husband? No children?

Rick bought me blue glass bangles, rough edged, with bubbles floating in the thick glass. He put them on my wrist, four of them stacked one on top of the other. I fondled the bracelets but what I wanted was his hand between my legs.

We sat for hours with the merchant. He showed us rugs and jewelry and silk scarves. Rick showed me the teapots, repaired with silver staples. The hashish finally came out. Bricks of it, stamped with a gold seal in one corner. Rick smiled and made his deal. Oliver watched.

When we left, it was dark, the hashish wrapped in newspaper and tied with string. Rick unpacked it in the room and we saw it was nothing but newspaper, folded over into the shape of a brick, and he laughed and laughed.

"I've been buggered," he said. And I laughed too. I told him about Ray who got through Spanish customs from Morocco with a kilo that turned out to be pressed camel shit.

"You've been cheated," Oliver said. "You've been made a fool of. You might have simply thrown your money in the street."

Rick flashed his white teeth. "That's business, mate. That's the East for you," he said, and sat down to roll a five-paper English joint.

I thought it would never end, never change. I knew that Rick had a job waiting in Delhi and a girl back home. I had cast my lot with Oliver, who was taking me to Goa as though I were a package, even though I was unraveling bit by bit.

But when we got to Kabul, the mood darkened. Rick found a hotel and we put down our bags as we had done in every hotel since the Amir Kabir except that this time Rick didn't put down his bag.

"I'll be at the Mustafa," he said to me, as though Oliver were not there, as though Oliver didn't exist, and he walked out. I sat down on the bed.

"You're not leaving too, are you?" Oliver said, the first words he had spoken to me directly since Istanbul.

"Why would I?" I said.

"Don't. Please," he said, but I was already out the door. I was a horse at the starting gate. I was a nervous filly.

I took him in my arms and we lay down on one of the beds and twined our arms and legs and I let him make love to me. He kissed my neck and I turned my head to face the door, wondering how long I would have to wait before I could leave for the Mustafa Hotel.

I held him for as long as I could bear and then I got up, got dressed and left. I didn't think about the future, the plan I had schemed that very first night, to have Oliver take me to India, to Goa for Christmas.

"I knew you would come," Rick said, and we took a bath together in the first tub I had seen since Europe. And then we slept, until, at 4:00 A.M., there was a knock on the door.

It was Oliver. He stood there, arms hanging, his beautiful silky hair matted, his beautiful face dirty and wet with tears. Did I feel for him? Did I want to comfort him? Did I care what had happened?

No, I wanted him to go away. I wanted to shut the door in his face. I wanted him to disappear, but he came into the room. He got into the bed between us. Like sentries we lay on either side of him and listened to him cry. Rick and I looked at each other over his body as it shook with his sobbing.

He told us he'd gone to a café for tea. He said a group of Afghan men had invited him to sit with them. They had bought him a meal. They asked him if he wanted to smoke hashish and he said yes and got into a car with them. They drove into the desert, they smoked hashish with him, and then, he said, they raped him, one by one, over the hood of the car.

"Afghan custom," they told him, laughing, having a good time with this beautiful boy, this boy who was as beautiful as a girl. I imagined his beauty was not lost on them. I imagined they felt lucky.

We knew that, for a woman, for a wife, to raise a bride price, the men would have to wait a long time. They would be middle-aged by then, but here, fallen so easily into their midst was a beautiful boy who looked like a girl. I don't imagine Oliver resisted. He said there were many of them. I don't imagine they were gentle.

"No bad feeling," the one who spoke English had said to him. "Afghan custom," they all repeated. He said they dropped him in the city and pressed a small square of hashish into his palm and they drove off. The hashish was still in his hand when he came to our hotel.

"We have to tell someone," I said. "The police, the embassy. Oliver, you have to see a doctor."

Oliver lay on his side between us, choosing to face Rick, silent. Rick said he would find them. He wanted answers. Where had he met them? Where had they dropped him off? How many? What did they look like?

I saw he was offended, affronted, one of his tribe, of men, of Englishmen, had been violated. He wanted revenge. He wanted to act like a man.

"Just let me lie here," Oliver said and he fell asleep, like a child, our child, and we watched over him, Rick and I, until dawn.

They left together in the morning. Oliver leaning on Rick's arm, his face washed clean. I watched from the window as they got into a minibus in the square in front of the hotel that would take them through the Khyber Pass and into Pakistan, into Peshawar. They would cross the border into India together, at Rawalpindi, the two of them together.

I went the rest of the way on my own, hitching a ride with a trucker who I thought was going to rape and kill me and throw my body into a ravine when he stopped the truck and got out halfway through the Pass to take a piss.

I made it all the way to Delhi on trucks with engines that the Indian drivers repaired with hairpins and rubber bands. I rode in the box built on top of the cab of the truck and crouched low against the night wind. I traded my still-elegant Italian wool coat for cotton pajamas and made my way to Goa. It was almost Christmas.

Marguerite was there. She had made it to Goa before me. "Here is Paradise," she said when I found her. She had to leave the French boys, she told me. "I think maybe they are finished," she added and she shrugged.

Then she took me by the hand to her whitewashed house by the ocean and there, although she said she didn't want to be the first, put a needle in my arm. I lay back and closed my eyes. When I opened them again, Marguerite was standing over me.

"You see?" she said.

SIX AND FIVE

Santino wanted the good things in life. He had six suits and a dozen white linen handkerchiefs from a fancy store uptown, but he thought there must be more so he got married. To have it regular, he said.

Before he got married, he said, he couldn't get arrested. Before he got married, the only girl he had was BoBo Johnny's sister, and everybody had her. She smelled bad and didn't always know where she was.

Santino would lean her against the wall under the stairs where the super kept the ashcans. In summer Santino would take her out in the backyards of the tenement buildings and they would do it between the sheets. They would stand between the sheets hanging on the clotheslines and he would put it in. Sometimes the sheets were wet and sometimes they were dry. It depended what time of day they did it.

BoBo Johnny's sister would play a counting game on her fingers. She would hold them up and push them into Santino's face.

"How many fingers do I got?" she'd say.

"Ten, Teresa, you got ten fingers. Everybody's got ten fingers," he'd say.

"Eleven, I got eleven fingers. Ask me how, you. Ask me how."

"How, Teresa?"

It was hard for him to talk. It wasn't what he liked to do when he was putting it in.

"Watch, watch. I'll show you. Watch me!" She would hold up her hands and she would fold down her fingers, starting with the pinky of her right hand. "Ten . . . nine . . . eight . . . seven . . . six . . . ," she would count. "And five is eleven!" she would shout, her left hand square in his face, fingers spread. "Fooled you, fooled you!"

Santino would move against her. He'd put his mouth on her ear. "Teresa," he would say, his voice hoarse, low.

She would push away and lean back and put her hands in his face. "Hey, you," she'd say. "How many fingers do I got, huh? How many fingers?"

The girl Santino married, the girl he found to give it to him lying down and regular, was not a girl from the neighborhood. The girl Santino married had her own apartment, with pictures on the wall she told him were Picassos. All her shoes had high heels. She said she was a model and didn't need a church wedding. Santino didn't think to ask her why and hadn't known her long when he took her down to city hall.

He showed up home that day and told his mother to fold up the cot in the kitchen for good.

"I don't need it no more," Santino told her. "I got married." He smiled with half his mouth. "I got my own place now."

"Who is she?" Mama wanted to know.

Santino took his clothes out of the tin closet in the kitchen. He counted six suits and he hung them on the knob of the apartment door.

"She's not one of us, is she?" Mama said.

"Us, us, who's 'us'? Wait till you see her."

"I can wait," Mama said.

Santino took the suits off the knob of the door and opened it. He thought he heard Teresa counting under the stairs.

The girl Santino married had an apartment with a bathroom and a bedroom with a door. He lay on the bed in the bedroom for a long time looking at the pictures on the wall.

"Picasso," she said. "Picasso painted them just for me. We met in Spain. We had dinner in Paris. We swam at Biarritz." She told him she spoke Spanish; she spoke French.

These must be the good things, Santino thought. He blessed his good fortune. He would have it lying down and regular with a woman who could talk French.

The girl Santino married didn't go modeling anymore. She went out in the day and sometimes at night. A woman came on Tuesdays to clean.

Santino drove a truck in the day and tended bar at night. He bought himself another suit, sharkskin. He ate dinner in the restaurant where he worked.

The girl Santino married was always sleeping when he came home. She told him she needed a car and he went to work on the weekends. And no, she couldn't meet his mother. She said it was too far downtown and not her kind of neighborhood.

One Sunday Santino went alone to see his mother. He put on the sharkskin suit. He put a white linen handkerchief and a fifty-dollar bill in his jacket pocket. The fifty was to stake his mother. He took the subway because the girl he married needed the car.

Teresa was outside on the stoop when Santino got there.

"Hello, Teresa," Santino said.

Someone had braided her hair and pinned it up. There was chocolate around her mouth and the laces were missing from one of her shoes.

"Sit with me," she said, and moved over.

Santino took out his white linen handkerchief and spread it out on the step next to her and sat down. Teresa took his hands in hers.

"I can't stay long, Teresa. I come to see my mama. You know I don't live here no more," Santino said.

Teresa let his hands drop into her lap. Santino could smell her. The girl he married didn't smell at all.

"Teresa," he said.

He took her under the stairs and then out into the backyard between the sheets and then he took her to Sam & Al's and bought her fifty dollars' worth of candy. Al said there wasn't that much candy in the store and that Teresa should take some comic books.

"She can't read," Santino said. "You know that."

"Let her look at the pictures," Al said.

Santino said for Al to give her credit. Al took his black-and-white notebook with the pencil tied to it with string from behind the register and on a clean page wrote down: "Teresa Sant'Angelo—$40 credit."

"Show it to her," Santino said.

"You said she can't read."

"Show it to her anyway."

Teresa looked at the page and traced the words with her finger. When she was done Al put the book back behind the register. Teresa took her ten-dollar bag of candy and went back to sit on the stoop. Santino's white linen handkerchief was still there and she pushed it out into the street with her foot.

Santino thought that she would ask him to sit down next to her again and he would have to tell her that he couldn't, not without the handkerchief. But Teresa didn't ask him. She just sat there, her hands around the bag of candy.

"You happy, Teresa?" Santino said. "You ever see so much candy?"

Teresa emptied the bag out onto the stoop. The pieces of candy were wrapped in colored cellophane and twisted at the ends. She lined them up along the top step where the handkerchief had been. When the top step was full, she slid down to the next step and the next until the stoop was covered with candy pieces. She counted them. She started at the top step and counted the candies backward from eleven.

"You know what, Teresa?" he said. "I'm getting out of here. You won't see me no more, you or my mama. You know where I'm going, Teresa? I'm going to Vegas. Vegas is in the desert, Teresa, and out there they know how to live. Blinky Manero's out there. He always said I should go out there. Said for me to look him up, that he could help me get my hand into something. Blinky done good out there, married a showgirl." Santino sniggered, cupping his hands in front of his chest when he said the word "showgirl." "Everybody drives big cars out there in Vegas, Teresa. They drive them with the tops down because it never rains. I bet you didn't know that, did you? That it never rains in Vegas. That's where I'm going, for sure. You won't see me down here no more."

Teresa was at the bottom step. She finished counting the pieces of candy and then she climbed back to the top and started to count them again.

JAMES DEAN AND ME

We got to the border late. Too late to cross, they told us. Well, not exactly. But the Afghans would not let us in because it was their dinnertime, and then they would have their coffee and a smoke, and probably even if we bribed them they wouldn't check us through. We would have to spend the rest of the night in the patch of no-man's-land in the desert, and if they got angry at us for some reason—because we had disturbed their dinner or disturbed their coffee or their smoke—they might not let us in at all. We would have to go back and that might not be possible because the Iranians were very sensitive about accepting people back that the Afghans had rejected. We could understand, certainly.

I looked at James. He looked at me. We decided to stay. The border guard smiled. He should not have, not with those black broken teeth that showed when he did, but who can control mirth? He told us that, conveniently enough, there was a hotel and restaurant just a furlong away with everything we could possibly need. James, of course, needed nothing, having been dead for some time. I liked him that way. He was just as handsome as when he was alive, which was amazing when you considered that terrible car crash.

James didn't even resent that people paid money to see the wreck.

He had heard that they had rigged it up so that it smoked all the time, as though the crash had just happened, and this made people very excited. They felt like they were right there. There were plans to preserve his body and maybe have it thrown across the seat in such a way that you could see his face, which was perfectly fine, not a scratch. The studio discussed messing it up a bit—some blood here, a cut there. One of the studio executives even suggested that they might remove an eye. That would really fascinate the crowd, he said (Jimmy did have such beautiful blue eyes). But in the end they thought it was too much trouble and went with just the smashed-up car.

Well, was I glad. First off, I never would have met James, and second, if I had, he would have been a mess, and as much as I'm in love with his personality, it's his physical being that gets me, especially those beautiful blue eyes. He never explained to me how he got to Teheran. We found each other across the street from the Amir Kabir in a coffee shop where they served that thick sweet coffee and tea in little glass cups. I had been sitting in there alone when he came in. I knew who he was right off. He sat down next to me. He said he didn't know why.

The first thing I said to him was, "You're James Dean, aren't you?"

He had looked at me like I was crazy. "Are you crazy?" he'd said. "Do you know how long James Dean has been dead?"

"Maybe," I'd said. "Maybe not."

"But he died in that terrible car crash. The Porsche, remember?"

"I remember."

"Anyway, what would James Dean be doing here in Teheran?"

I'd shrugged. "What do I know? You should know. You're James Dean."

It had been his turn to shrug. We shared a pot of tea and left together. He had this great hotel room and we stayed there until our visas were ready to run out and we had to move on.

So there we were at the border. The name on James's passport was Kevin Muldooney. Of course, he couldn't travel under his own name. I understood that. The first time I saw his passport, he started to say something about the name, but I'd put a finger to his lips. I didn't want to know anything. After all, some things you just don't question. His name didn't matter. I knew who he was.

The border hotel was cooler than I expected. James had different expectations. It was complicated. We were more than a generation apart even though we were both twenty-four. (There is definitely an advantage to dying young, never ever having to grow old.) And don't forget, he was a movie star.

There were a lot of other travelers at the hotel. French, Dutch, German, even a couple of guys from South America . . . Argentina, I think it was. One of them was old but really well built and handsome and tan. He was half-naked even though the desert was so cold at night. He was wearing leather pants and had on some kind of feather-and-bead necklace with a matching headband. He was telling a story of getting beat up in Turkey and his friend Paco had a black eye and cuts on his nose, as if to back up the story. I heard something about Pamplona and Hemingway and I went "Wow" like the rest of the travelers who could understand English, but whispered to James that I wanted to get out of there.

• • •

The next morning we went to the coffee shop and tried to find out about the bus to the border, but no one could tell us anything. Everyone was sitting around drinking tea and coffee and smoking huge standing water pipes.

"Now what?" I said to James.

"Hey, what do we care?" he said. "Cool out. When a bus shows up, we'll leave."

"But we're on the edge of no-man's-land. We could be here forever."

James shrugged, leaned over, and gave me a kiss. I could see one of the Iranians watching us. Sometimes they cut holes in the walls or peered through the keyhole or just put their ear up against the door of the room where we slept. They thought we were all insatiable sexual animals and they wanted us desperately but were afraid to ask.

So the morning passed, and everyone started ordering lunch. I'd cooled out like James said. He was holding my hand under the table when this European man came into the café. He stuck out like a sore thumb. He was tall and very blond, very white. I thought he was in his sixties, but it was hard to tell. We were all so young that everyone who wasn't as young as we were looked very old. I remember how dignified he was. His hair was short and smooth and parted to one side, and he wore a suit, an expensive European suit, with a tie and gold cuff links. He came right over to our table and sat down.

"Please," he said, "I need your help."

He looked from me to James and back again. He leaned over the table. I was worried that a sleeve of that beautiful suit would go into one of the empty cups of coffee and be stained forever by the sticky syrup at the bottom of the cup, but it didn't. He leaned even closer, put his face next to ours, and folded his hands on the table.

"Will you help me?" he said.

"Who are you?"

"Shhh." He had an accent . . . Scandinavian, I thought, and I was right.

"I'm with the Swedish Embassy in Kabul."

"Great, maybe you can get us out of here and across the border. We got here last night and . . ."

James put a toothpick in his mouth and sat back, real slumped, like he always did for his publicity photos. God, was I in love. I forgot all about the Swedish diplomat and just concentrated on James.

"I'm trying to save a girl, an American girl."

James was quiet and so was I, but James was watching the Swede. I was watching James, his beautiful blue eyes, his beautiful face, his beautiful hair. I was wondering how he got his hair to stay like that all the way out here in the desert. His hair looked exactly like it did in all his photos.

"I have to convince the authorities to let this girl go, or she'll spend the rest of her life in the insane asylum. Have you any idea what an insane asylum is like in Afghanistan?"

James held my hand against the muscle in his thigh.

"Imagine a dark pit dug into the ground," the Swede said.

"That's it?"

"That's it . . . and a bucket to do your business and the food, they throw it down at you—maggoty pieces of bread and lamb fat that dogs have chewed on." The Swede closed his eyes. "That poor girl." He opened his eyes. "She's from Connecticut."

"Oh, my God," I said. "What can we do?"

"You can save her."

"How?"

"I can't go into details here. It's not safe. You have to trust me." His blue eyes bored into James's blue eyes. "Will you help me? Will you come?"

"Of course I will," I said, jumping up, upsetting a teapot. The Swede caught it before it could shatter, but not before the tea spilled out over the table. I remember watching the puddle of tea form on the table when I heard the Swede say, "Not you . . . him."

"Why just him?" I said. The lamb kebab I'd had for lunch went sour in my stomach.

"Because he's James Dean," the Swede whispered. "They'll listen to him."

"I don't know," I said. "I don't like it. We've been together since . . ."

The Swede ignored me. He put his hand, a very big hand with pink nails, on James's shoulder. "Will you come? Will you save the American girl?"

James stood up, took his comb out of his hip pocket, and ran it through his hair. "Let's go," he said.

"James . . ."

"I'll be back in no time, sweetheart. Be cool."

I waved goodbye, but he didn't see me. The Swede had an arm around his shoulders; it was almost an embrace. "I'll wait right here," I said. "I'll be right here waiting."

When I walked to the door of the café and looked out into the desert, I saw a black Volvo in the distance. I sat in the coffee shop until it was dark and they made me leave. I went back to the hotel. It was empty now because everyone else had somehow found the bus to the border. More travelers arrived the next night, caught in the wheel of no-man's-land—Afghanistan closed, nice hotel, nice restaurant, you spend the night—and I sat with them in the café until they, too, caught the bus to the border.

The manager at the hotel tried to convince me to share my room because there were so many travelers coming through, all trying to beat the summer season when typhoid and cholera would close the border, but I said I was waiting for James, and he'd be back in no time, and then he wouldn't have a place to stay.

A month passed before I left the border hotel. The Iranians were starting to look at me funny. Even the boy who cleaned my room and watched me through the keyhole said it was time for me to go. There was talk that I was working for SAVAK. I didn't want to disappear in no-man's-land.

Before I left, I went into the café and asked everyone about the Swedish diplomat and the American girl from Connecticut being held prisoner in an Afghan insane asylum. News traveled fast on the road. There were people in the café coming from both directions across the border, and I'd hoped someone might tell me something.

"He left in a black Volvo. He took James Dean with him," I said.

"Who?"

"James Dean. Jimmy. Jimmy Dean. You know. *Rebel Without a Cause*. Natalie Wood. *Giant*. The Porsche. 'Die young and leave a beautiful corpse.'"

"Far out . . . James Dean . . . ," someone said. The smoke from the water pipes was so thick I could hardly see who was talking.

"You're crazy, man," I heard a voice say. "James Dean? He's dead."

"He's not," I told him. "He's just missing."

"I remember a girl, in Erzurum, in Turkey. She got off the bus and walked into the mountains, and no one ever saw her again."

"Cool," from the crowd.

"I heard about her. She was a French teacher from New Jersey."

"Wow!" from the crowd.

I took the bus to the border and asked about James and the Swede and the American girl as I passed through Herat and Kandahar and Kabul, and over the Khyber Pass into Peshawar and Rawalpindi. I even went to the Swedish Embassy when I got to New Delhi. I spoke to a tall blond man who said Sweden had no embassy in Afghanistan, and he was sorry about my boyfriend, but, after all, did we think we could go traipsing around the world with no money and no purpose and expect our embassies to bail us out when we got into trouble?

"No," I said. "Of course not, but you have to understand. This is not just my boyfriend. This is James Dean."

He got me a chair and a glass of water. "I think you should know," he said very gently. "James Dean is dead."

I sipped the water. My mouth was dry. "I know," I told him. "I hate to believe it, but you're probably right."

MALAFEMMENA

· There was very little Tom could tell you about Lucia. She had bowled him over, knocked him for a loop, taken his breath away, and truth be told, taken him for a ride. This is what Marianna would have said and she didn't even know the whole story. It was the *colpo di fulmine*. The lightning bolt. That first time Tom saw her, his goose was cooked.

The Setting: Abbondanza's on the Bay, temple to Italian American excess in Queens. The wedding reception of Annemarie Montepulciano who had hooked a dentist, or as her mother explained it, chopping at her neck with one hand, at her forehead with the other, "a doctor from here to there."

The Player: Tom could have cared less about Annemarie Montepulciano and her doctor from here to there but Mamone had asked him to go to the wedding. She wanted to stay home on Thompson Street but she also wanted her envelope delivered in person. More than that she wanted Tom to show himself, to show himself off—*la bella figura*. She wanted everyone to see him, and though it's hard to believe given her adoration, she wanted him to find a nice girl. After all, she told him a million times, she wouldn't live forever.

• • •

It was the cocktail hour. Abbondanza's on the Bay was famous for its cocktail hour. Chefs in high hats carved filet mignon and racks of lamb, servers in satin tuxedos opened littleneck clams and Long Island oysters, wielded tongs dangling king crab legs, and plucked whole Maine lobsters from ice sculptures of Mount Vesuvius. Blue flames warmed silver trays of baked ziti, fettuccine Alfredo, eggplant parmigiana; calamari swam in black ink.

On the other side, Mamone had told him, we ate olive oil on bread and sold our votes for a pound of rigatoni. She had also told him that she wanted no part of the old country. Good riddance, she always said, which was how Tom felt about Italian girls and their mothers.

He was standing near the entrance looking over the crowd of guests, the huge women in black sequins, flesh spilling over the backs of their dresses, cleavages that began at their chins. They watched their daughters, girls with exotically blackened eyes and blood-red mouths, diamonds in their ears, two or three to a lobe. They were beautiful, these girls, still slim, luscious in bandage dresses and expensive shoes, with pearly toes and loud laughs. They gathered in clumps, talking, talking, talking. The young men who held their futures stood at the edges of the room, slicked black hair, elegant Italian suits, gold jewelry. They smoked cigarettes and cracked their knuckles. Whatever happened, they would not dance.

Tom had been to Abbondanza's more times than he wanted to remember. It was the thing he did for Mamone, his link to that life he kept pushing back against. Abbondanza's was popular with the Staten Island and Brooklyn crews who had married at football weddings in rented halls on Houston Street, weddings where sandwiches—made on rolls shaped like footballs and wrapped in wax paper—were piled high on folding tables and thrown, like footballs, to guests. They lusted after an Abbondanza event. They had always partied, crammed together in rooms with trays of cold cuts and bakery cookies on lacy paper doilies, but now, having come up in the world, they wanted extravaganzas that ended with cotton candy machines and dessert carts decorated with sparklers, buckling under trays of miniature pastries and fruit cut into flower arrangements.

He first saw her standing next to the rack of lamb station. He had been getting a drink, planning his exit, and there she was, all bare arms and legs in terrifyingly high heels and a close-fitting white satin dress, a diamond at her neck and a string of them around her wrist. She was luminescent, iridescent, ethereal, and wearing the forbidden white dress. To wear white was to steal the bride's thunder. Everyone knew that. She was stealing the bride's thunder. What a bitch.

Tom couldn't look away. The *colpo di fulmine*. He recognized it, recognized her. She reminded him of the Madonna, not the blue-veiled one with downcast eyes, but the black one of the Mezzogiorno, the fertility goddess of the South.

At that moment, Mamone, sitting in the window on Thompson Street, her elbows resting on a folded-over bed pillow set on the sill, felt an ache in her heart and put a hand to her chest. She cursed fate before she went over to the alcove in the kitchen where a candle burned in front of her saint, and angry, she turned the statue to face the wall.

Tom watched the woman in the white dress go through the glass doors onto the narrow deck overlooking the water. He could see her out there in the dark, smoking, the orange tip of her cigarette glowing when she took a drag. And then she was gone. Just like that.

He filled a plate from the buffet tables but he wasn't hungry. He was, as always, both repelled and impressed at the amount of food. He looked and looked but the woman in the white dress had truly disappeared. A pain was starting in his right temple and then the band struck up "Here Comes the Bride." Clouds of white smoke rose from buckets of dry ice and when the smoke cleared, a glass elevator festooned with garlands of flowers came up through an opening in the floor. Inside were Annemarie Montepulciano and the doctor from here to there. The band switched to Sinatra, the MC announced that the couple was appearing for the first time as man and wife. "And here they are," he shouted into the microphone, making a sweeping gesture with his free hand, "Dr. and Mrs. . . ." Annemarie's mother swooned. The women mobbed the couple and cheered. The married men sat, the young studs stood against the wall, cigarettes hanging defiantly from their bottom lips.

Annemarie broke away from her groom, and clutching the white *busta* that had been made to match her dress, she circulated, accepting kisses and shoving envelopes into the bag she would give to her mother at the end of the night to make a record of who gave what. Tom saw an opening, an opportunity to hand over the envelopes and made his move. He knew Annemarie had no idea who he was but she smiled anyway, and stuffing the envelopes into the bag bursting with them, she moved on, the exchange of cash, even sealed in an envelope, always embarrassing in some small way.

He suddenly felt dizzy. He felt cold, then hot. He had a moment of fear. The woman in the white dress was standing next to him, curling her fingers around his arm. "You have a car?" she said, her accent heavy. He wasn't the least surprised.

"No, I . . ."

"Come with me," she said, and led him outside where she gave the valet her parking chit and a fifty-dollar bill. She took a pack of cigarettes from her purse, tapped it against her hand, and held the pack out to Tom. He took one though he hadn't smoked in years. The valet pulled up in a white Cadillac convertible; the red leather interior still smelled of the showroom. They got in.

"In Italy," she said, "I have a fast car, but here . . ." She shrugged her shoulders and, after a few puffs, threw the lit cigarette into the street. She drives like a lunatic, Tom thought, as they crossed into Manhattan. With one palm on the steering wheel she turned onto Laight Street, parked by a fire hydrant, and gestured for him to follow and he did. He followed her into the lobby of a building and into the elevator that opened at the fifth floor onto a loft. A small dog ran toward them barking and bit Tom's ankle, tearing a hole in his monogrammed silk sock.

"The dog . . . ," she said. "He bites. He's very jealous. Aren't you, Cicile?" She laughed low in her throat, scooped the dog up and kissed it square on its snout. Tom thought to tell her the socks were a gift from his boss, Curly, the host of the most successful show on daytime television, but he kept quiet.

"Lucia," she said, holding out her hand. Tom took her hand and held it.

"Tom . . ."

"*Bravo*," she said. He loved her voice. He loved her accent. He loved her.

She told him to sit down and she opened a bottle of wine. The loft was almost empty, bare of clues. High ceilings, two walls of uncovered windows. There were a table and chairs, a bed, a chest of drawers with a photo of Lucia on the back of a Vespa, holding on to a good-looking young man with curly dark hair, her arms around his waist, her head thrown back. A Cinzano ad, Tom thought, or a Neapolitan purse-snatching team in Spaccanapoli. He had another moment of fear.

They drank the wine and smoked her cigarettes, stubbing them out in a Murano glass ashtray the size of a cereal bowl while Cicile nestled in her lap. She had kicked off her shoes and put her feet up on his chair. Tom told her he was a television producer, that his grandmother had raised him not far from here. Lucia told him nothing.

When the wine was finished, she stood up and told him it was time for him to go. She called the elevator. The dog barked. Tom was waiting for the elevator when she came beside him and slid a hand around his waist. Her other hand covered his mouth. She kissed the side of his neck. A hand moved up his back and through his hair. She twisted his ear like a grade school nun. "When will I see you again?" he said, through her fingers, his saliva like wet fur in his mouth. She pulled away, backed him into the open elevator, and the doors closed.

Tom showed up in the production offices the next morning to Curly Crapanzano screaming for him in the studio. Marianna handed Tom the clipboard. "Welcome to *Life Is Just a Bowl of Cherries*," she said. "The cannoli of daytime television is looking for you, his producer and right-hand man."

"He'll have to settle for you," Tom said. He adjusted her headphones, handed back the clipboard. "I'm turning off my cell. Don't call."

"Are you kidding? You just got here—late, no less. What's going on with you? Drank too much at the ginzo wedding? Went home with Teresa Twelve-Vowels?" She made the face that reminded Tom of Mamone, the face that made interns tear up their ID tags and leave the building along with any idea of a career in daytime TV.

"I should marry you, Marianna," Tom said.

"I don't think so. I still haven't ruled out the possibility that you're gay."

"Your mother's ass," he said.

He took the stairs, two at a time, and on the way down he could hear Curly bellowing. Show Biz. Mamone was so proud of him. She told everyone that he worked in show business. "When I'm gonna get you Oscars?" she'd ask whenever he came to see her. ". . . in the curio cabinet. Here. I got a space here." Tom's Oscars were two daytime Emmys stuffed in a gym bag in his closet. Next time, he always promised, and always forgot.

Out on the street he bought a pack of cigarettes, sat on a park bench, and smoked them one after another. When he got back the studio was in chaos. Marianna reported that the woman whose son had burned down the family trailer and sold his blind brother's service dog for meth was crying in the green room. The boy was missing. How could Curly put this unhappy family's life back on track if they couldn't find him? The mother said the boy had disappeared right after she ordered drinks and burgers from room service.

"Room service?" Tom said. "They have room service in the Howard Johnson Motor Inn on Forty-Third Street?"

"I'm just repeating what she said," Marianna told him. "Let's just do the show without him. He could be dead, or living happily in the local Motel 6 in Podunk by now, having negotiated a monthly rate."

"You should find something else to do," Tom said.

"Plan B: we grab a kid with dirty hair off the street. Give

him a few bucks and pass him off as the son."

"Are you crazy?"

"Come on, Tom. It's all bullshit. When the show is over, Mom is going back to butt-fuck Ohio, picking up a family-size bag of Doritos and plunking her fat ass in front of the large plasma-screen TV that we paid for."

"I don't think daytime TV is your calling. I suggest law school."

"That's my sister, remember? She's the smart one?"

"Can you please just do your job and find Jimmy Tidewell? I'm leaving."

"You're going to get fired. This is your segment. You're pretty, Tom, but not that pretty. Your next gig could be waiting tables in a red sauce restaurant on Mulberry Street."

"It could be a blessing," he said over his shoulder on the way out.

Tom didn't want to go home that night so he went to Mamone's. She smoothed his hair and coaxed him to eat, covering the kitchen table with small plates the way he liked. *Poverino,* she called him, and kissed his forehead a hundred times. He noticed a new ex-voto hanging from her saint, a silver boy that he knew was a representation of him. She sent him off with food wrapped in tinfoil that he brought in to Marianna who had an Italian mother who didn't cook. Curly Crapanzano had noticed nothing. The show went on.

It was late on Saturday night when Tom's phone rang and went straight to voicemail. He listened to the message. Come to me. *Subito.* It was Lucia. He hadn't given her his number. He went, right away.

Tom stood outside Lucia's building. Laight Street was deserted. He went into the lobby, into the elevator and pushed the button for her floor. The elevator door opened into the loft and there they were, Lucia lifting that beautiful Murano glass ashtray, pink, shot through with tiny bubbles, curved like the wing of a bird. She held it high above her head, and she crashed it down onto the man's skull with such force that Tom lost his breath.

The man fell and lay still, his limbs contorted, blood seeping from the gash behind his ear. Lucia threw up her hands. "*Ma'nudge!*" she said, the words clipped in the way of Neapolitans and their dialect, their impatience with life. She kicked at the body, raised one finely shaped leg as though to stab a stiletto heel into the nearest wide-open staring eye. It would crack like an egg.

"Stop."

She did. Miraculously, Tom thought. She didn't look at Tom but turned away, sat down in a straight-backed chair facing the bloody scene and flung curses at the body on the floor.

"For Chrissakes. For Chrissakes . . . ," Tom said.

Lucia looked up. She was leaning forward in the chair, elbows on her knees, her legs apart, her skirt stretched high and tight. "What?" she said.

"Omigod . . . look at this! Do something. Hurry up!" Tom grabbed a kitchen towel and held it to the wound. Blood was pooling around the man's head.

Lucia watched him, her eyes hooded. "He's dead, no?"

"Dead . . . dead . . . Jesus, God, what do I know? I've never seen a dead body. Mamone covered my eyes at wakes." And put Vaseline in his nose, he remembered. Mamone would put Vaseline in each nostril with her little finger to block the smell of death and the overpowering scent of the flowers twisted into towers around the coffin.

Lucia came over and squatted by the body. She held two fingers to the man's neck and she made a sound like a hum, then took her two fingers and closed his eyes. She made the sign of the cross.

"Oh, God . . . oh, God . . . ," Tom said, watching her. "He's dead? . . . Call the police! Now . . . now . . . we have to call the police!"

Lucia looked over at him. "Shut up," she said, "and sit down."

Tom did. He sat in the straight-backed chair she had just vacated but he turned it sideways, away from the body, facing the windows . . . twelve big windows facing Laight Street. Had anyone seen?

But Laight Street was silent and dark, an invisible street. Tom had always known Laight Street as a short, narrow strip buried in the factory district, too far out of the heart of the neighborhood. Mamone had lived on this street as a young bride, in a building so derelict it was memorable.

Lucia took out her phone and Tom relaxed. "911 . . . call 911," he told her, because how would she know? She was a foreigner; he was taking no chances. He told himself it would be OK. He'd be back in his own apartment in no time. And tomorrow he'd be back at work, telling the story to Marianna. Tom thought it would be simple. Tom was a fool.

"*Si. Capisco. Certo. Bene. Grazie. Aspetto qui. Non ti preoccupato. Ciao . . . ciao!*"

"You got an operator who speaks Italian?" Tom said.

"My uncle."

"Your uncle? Your uncle? At 911?"

"Stop being stupid. Not a real uncle. An uncle from Rome . . . you don't know this? Your Mamone, nothing she taught you?" Lucia turned away. "I will make some coffee," she said. "You sit. Talk. Tell me something amusing."

She went to the kitchen and stood at the counter, pouring coffee beans into the grinder. She filled the pot and set it on the stove. Together they drank coffee and waited. He couldn't think of one amusing thing to tell her.

The uncle arrived and Tom thought he looked familiar. Lucia kissed him on both cheeks. He nodded at Tom and moved toward the body. Lucia came up behind the uncle and put a hand on his shoulder. The uncle took an oversized white handkerchief from his back pocket and wiped his forehead. He was not a big man but he was sweating like one. Mamone would say he was sweating like a horse. He and Lucia put their heads together. They spoke in low voices, so Tom couldn't hear; they spoke in Italian, so Tom wouldn't understand.

When the uncle picked up his head, he motioned to Tom to come over to where he stood with Lucia. "Joe," he said, crushing Tom's hand. Then, "Wait, wasn't you at my niece Annemarie's wedding? She married the doctor? Annemarie Montepulciano? Yeah." Joe didn't wait for an answer. "Let's go," he said. "Let's get this guy outta here."

"What?"

Joe blew air through his lips. "We got to move this guy. I can't do it on my own."

"Wait. Aren't we calling the police?" Tom was the one sweating now. Silence. "Listen, I don't know what's going on here but I really think we should call the police. This guy was trying to kill her!" He looked at the beautiful Lucia. "Tell him. Tell him what happened." But she only stared, her eyes like black moons.

"What's your name, kid?"

"Tom."

"Nice to meet you, Tommy. But to tell you the truth? No. We ain't calling the police. But listen, I don't want you getting the wrong idea. This here's not my line of work. I'm a contractor . . . but when things gotta get done, they gotta get done, you know? Now, be a man and help me out." He turned to Lucia. "You got a rug, honey? A shower curtain? Something we can wrap him up in?"

They laid the quilt from Lucia's bed on the floor and lined it with garbage bags before they rolled the body into the center. They wrapped it with four colored stretch ropes with hooks on the ends that Lucia had taken from a suitcase in the corner. A greaseball's suitcase, Tom thought, watching her. He didn't want to look down at the mummy lying at his feet.

Joe stood up complaining about his back. Lucia sat down and lit a cigarette. "*Cazzo*," she said. "I should not have left Italy."

Joe shook his head. "Your husband's not going to like this when he hears."

"Husband?" Tom said. "You have a husband?"

Lucia shrugged. "In Italy . . . ," she said, and exhaled, the smoke curling up into her nose and back out her mouth. "I have many things in Italy."

"Let's go, kid. I don't wanna be here all night."

They lifted the body into the elevator. Lucia stood in the doorway.

"My truck is just outside," Joe said, when they reached the lobby. "Wait here. Hold the elevator. Close the door quick if somebody comes."

Tom panicked. "You think somebody's going to come?"

"Jesus, kid. What? I got a crystal ball? Just hold the elevator. Anybody comes, I'll take care of it." Joe left and Tom was alone with the body. He didn't want to touch it, not even with the tip of his shoe. He planted his feet along the edge of the elevator and put his hands against the wall to steady himself, one finger on the button holding the door open. He shut his eyes and prayed that no one would come.

Joe's truck was lipstick red with flames painted along the sides. "She's a beauty, no?" Joe said. "I love this truck. I take good care of it, like a woman." He winked at Tom. Before they heaved the body into the back, Joe insisted on lining the truck bed with burlap bags he said he used to carry cement. "Even with the plastic," he told Tom, "you never know what could leak out." The two of them were breathing hard and sweating like horses when Joe finally pulled up the back panel of the truck. Tom made to leave, but Joe took hold of his arm. "Whoa, cowboy. We're not finished yet," he said. "Relax." Tom vomited in the street while Joe waited, the passenger door swung open, and then gave him mints from the glove compartment. "I know you're nervous, kid. You think I ain't nervous? But you get shit on your shoe, you clean it off, you know? You gotta be a man."

They drove through the streets, into the Brooklyn-Battery Tunnel, over the Verrazano Bridge, into the darkness of Staten Island, on roads with no lights, then no houses, until Joe pulled up in front of a cyclone fence. He opened the gates, got back in the truck and drove inside. "Get one of them dollies," Joe told him, pointing at a wall of equipment, "and bring it over here. I'm not carrying this *judrool* one more step. Then all we gotta do is tip him into one of these here containers." Tom got out of the car, and started to gag. "Geez, kid. You got something wrong with your stomach? I know you got something wrong with your head, getting mixed up with that broad Lucia."

Tom wanted to ask him what he meant. He wanted to ask Joe who Lucia really was, what she was doing here, why she was at Annemarie Montepulciano's wedding, but instead he took the white handkerchief Joe handed him ("I always carry two") and wiped his mouth.

"Thanks. It's the smell," Tom said. "Christ, what is it?"

"Who the hell knows? Some kind of toxic waste."

"Toxic waste?"

"Yeah, be careful. You're young yet, you don't wanna have no two-headed babies. Hey, it's a joke." He punched Tom's shoulder. "But for real, don't touch nothing . . . the guys work in here, they wear those space suits, you know?"

"Hazard suit?"

"Yeah, whatever."

"Toxic waste?"

"Yeah, perfect, no? We get this guy into one of these containers and that's the end of it. Bye-bye. Next stop, Africa."

"Africa?"

"Hey. There's big money in toxic waste. From what I hear, the Giambellis have it all sewed up."

"They send toxic waste from here to Africa?"

"Yeah. Why? You want it in your backyard?"

Joe let Tom off at St. George, the ferry terminal on the Staten Island side. He told him he could keep the handkerchief. Tom sat on the outside deck of the ferry, shivering, the wind pushing at him, stinging his eyes. When the ferry docked at the Whitehall terminal in downtown Manhattan, Tom got into a cab and passed out so that the driver had to shake him awake when they reached Thompson Street. "You OK, buddy?" he asked, when Tom gave him a twenty and told him to keep the change. "You had me scared for a minute. I thought for sure you were dead."

Mamone was asleep when he came in. The next morning she was surprised to see him there but happy in her heart. She went out early to shop for him after he said he was staying. She asked no questions but kissed the head of her saint before she left.

Tom stayed in bed at Mamone's for the rest of the day and the rest of the week, and the week after that. Mamone fed him and when she made his bed he got up and sat on the couch and watched daytime TV. At night, to fall asleep, he drank wine from the gallon jug Mamone kept in the kitchen. His cellphone rang and rang. It was Marianna, calling from the show. She left message after message: Where was he? What was he doing? Curly was going crazy . . .

Tom thought about nothing. He left a message for Marianna telling her the show looked good, she was doing a good job, and that maybe her sister wasn't the smart one after all.

It was two weeks later when he finally called Marianna back. "Jesus . . . ," she said. "Have you gone completely nuts? Where are you? I went over to the apartment and nothing, no sign of you." He'd forgotten she had his key. "In case you die," she had told him. "A lady in my building? They found her after ten days. She was stuck to the floor."

Tom said nothing. Marianna went on and on. He thought about hanging up, or at least covering his ears, like a child. He felt like a child. "So, you're not answering?" she said finally. "You're not going to tell me what's going on? You're on a suicide mission?"

"I'm not feeling good," Mamone heard him say and she came and sat next to him on the couch.

"You not feeling so good?" Mamone whispered. "Why you no say something? Who's that? That nice pretty girl works with you? Invite her over tonight. I got plenty." Tom made a face and Mamone desisted. She sat back further on the couch and scowled.

"I'll be OK," Tom told Marianna. "I just need some time."

"It's two weeks! You're definitely getting fired."

"Thanks. That's helpful."

"There's something else." Marianna lowered her voice. "These two detectives came to the studio looking for you. Tall, short. Good guy, bad guy. Curly was not happy. Why would detectives be looking for you? You're the biggest pussy I know. What do you have, some kind of secret life?"

"Marianna, I love you but I've got to go."

"And . . . ?"

"And what?"

"You're coming in?"

"Yes," he said. "Yes. Tomorrow. I'll be there. And I'll tell you everything."

The next morning, when Tom kissed Mamone goodbye he saw that the saint in the alcove had company, and all of the plaster statues were surrounded with votives and draped with rosebuds strung on twine. "You come tonight, Tommy?" Mamone said, touching his cheek.

"Yes, for sure. If you don't burn the house down first."

"Maybe you bring that nice girl?"

"Maybe, Mamone. Maybe."

"I got plenty."

Tom showed up at the Curly Crapanzano show shaved and dressed as though nothing had happened. He went into his office and sat behind his desk. He would wait, for Marianna, for Lucia, for the detectives. He would wait and someone would come and something would happen. He kept hearing Joe's words: "Be a man," he had said. "You gotta be a man."

LOUISE CIARELLI

When Father Linus came into St. Anthony's sixth-grade classroom and took the pins out of Louise Ciarelli's hair, pins that Sister Pauline had put there that very morning indicating that the mass of black curls that reached down her back were an occasion of sin and designed to tempt, we all gasped.

None of us thought this was inappropriate but we knew it was unkind. We were stunned, though we knew that priests trumped nuns, and Father Linus had no idea Sister Pauline had put those pins in Louise's hair herself right after the pledge of allegiance to the flag.

Sister Pauline was a huge German import, an oddity among the Irish nuns who both taught and loathed us. Sister Pauline called the dust bunnies that accumulated under our desk *schnitzels* and referred to us as *dummkopfs* when we gave the wrong answer or none at all and once slapped Lorraine Marchese so hard back and forth across the face for sitting sideways in her desk that Lorraine went deaf for the rest of the afternoon.

No use complaining. Our parents were united on this point. "You must have deserved it. You're lucky that's all you got." This is what we were told. Or worse, we got a matching slap for meriting the first one.

• • •

"You're so beautiful," Father Linus said to Louise, his hands caught in her hair as he lined up the hairpins one by one, side by side, on her desk. "Why would you put your hair up like this?" And he smiled at her.

Father Linus was young and handsome and Louise Ciarelli was three years older than the rest of us, having been left back twice before. She did manage to graduate but only because I let her copy off my paper during final exams.

I remember she wore spike heels with taps that made a sound when we climbed the steps of the church to get our diplomas. Her eyes were lined in drugstore black liquid eyeliner, winged at the corners, her lips pale, almost white, which was the fashion then. There was no question of her going to a real high school. She was almost seventeen.

Louise didn't say anything to Father Linus about Sister Pauline pinning up her hair. She just looked him straight in the eye, a real temptress, the perfect occasion of sin.

"Sister Pauline," Father Linus said, turning away.

"Yes, Father?" Sister Pauline lowered her eyes, deferentially. Weren't priests the representation of Jesus Christ himself on earth? Didn't they have those consecrated fingers?

"Anybody in this class giving you any trouble?" Father Linus asked. The moment of terror had arrived. Father Linus came to our classroom once a week as the supreme disciplinarian, the Grand Inquisitor, and a word from Sister Pauline meant humiliation in front of the whole class. It was always the boys who needed disciplining and if ever any of us enjoyed being a dame it was when Father Linus showed up.

• • •

"No, Father," Sister Pauline began. "They've been a good bunch except maybe for James over there, who was missing at Mass this Sunday. James Radiccio, stand up." She raised her voice when she said this, to make sure he knew it was an order.

"Is that true, James?" Father Linus said, making his way through the aisles of the forty-four polished, neatly lined-up desks, his brown Franciscan robe catching around his ankles, the crucifix of the black rosary hanging from the cord around his waist banging against his knees as he walked. He got to James, who was the smallest and the feistiest among us and always took his beatings without flinching, and we all flinched for him when Father Linus pulled him out of his seat by his ear. "So James, is the good Sister right? You missed Mass this Sunday?" He spun Jimmy around to face him and we could see Jimmy's pain, from the set of his mouth and the squint of his eyes. And we knew that Father Linus had not even begun.

"I went to Mass Sunday, Father. I did," Jimmy lied.

"But Sister says you weren't there, James. Would you be calling her a liar?" Father Linus twisted Jimmy's ear until we thought he would lift him off the floor. I imagined that when he finally let go, Jimmy would be suspended in air and we would have witnessed a miracle. We all held our breaths in hope and fear.

But then Louise Ciarelli stood up, that black hair falling over one eye, all the way down the front of her uniform, her breasts poking out the bib of her jumper, because that uniform wasn't designed for the likes of Louise Ciarelli, and she said, "Jimmy did go to Mass Sunday, Father. The eight o'clock. I was right behind him when we went up for Communion."

Father Linus turned away from Jimmy, but not before he pushed him back down into his seat, where Jimmy sat rubbing his ear, his upper lip raised in a sneer because he knew Father Linus's eyes were elsewhere.

• • •

"You don't say?" Father Linus said. Louise nodded. "But you know you're supposed to go to the nine o'clock, all together, the whole school. You know that, don't you? You are all obligated to attend the children's Mass." Louise ran a hand through her hair; we watched it fall back across her face. She stood, one arm holding the other, framing her breasts. She didn't look down.

"I know, Father," she said. "But we took our grandmothers. There was no one else to take them this Sunday. They go together, mine and Jimmy's, every Sunday to the eight o'clock. We live on Thompson Street, 194, me and Jimmy, across the hall from each other. We got up early Sunday so we could take them. Otherwise they would have missed. I wasn't at the nine o'clock either." Louise looked straight at Father Linus and then out at the class. "Ask anyone," she said. "They all saw us leaving when they were lined up outside."

"Is that so, James?" Father Linus walked over to Jimmy, who jumped out of his chair and stood up straight as a soldier.

"Yes, Father. That's the God's honest truth." Father Linus smacked him then, on the side of the head, for taking the Lord's name in vain, but that was a piece of cake compared to being marched to the front of the room and bent over Sister Pauline's desk.

We let out a collective sigh but it wasn't over yet. Was it ever? Father Linus went up and down the aisles and one by one we were made to stand and face him. "Did you see James Radiccio leaving the eight o'clock mass on Sunday?" he said. And one by one we answered, "Yes."

When Father Linus had canvased the entire class, he took his place at the front of the classroom while Sister Pauline glared at Louise and hissed for Jimmy to sit down. Father Linus began a prayer, admonishing us to be good Catholic boys and girls and to listen to Sister Pauline, who stood in the back of the room, under the flag, her hands folded inside the wide sleeves of her habit. We knew she would take care of Jimmy Radiccio later, and she did, for the rest of the year.

And Louise Ciarelli? After that morning nothing could touch or hurt her ever again. Sister Pauline pretended Louise wasn't in the classroom, and Louise, defiant, wore her hair loose over one eye, the skirt of her uniform high above her knees, and on Mondays, the day Father Linus came, she would line her eyes with the black liquid pen she had stolen from one of her four sisters.

She wanted to line my eyes too when I would go to her house for lunch. Instead we would watch *The Secret Storm*, a soap opera that came on at noon for fifteen minutes every weekday. The television was in the kitchen, and we'd watch it, Louise's four sisters and mother and grandmother and me, and eat escarole soup with fidelini and bread from Zito's on Bleecker Street.

We were friends, Louise and I. She was so beautiful and grown-up but would come to my house to play dolls, dress them in gorgeous clothes that my Aunt Irene made for me. My mother said Aunt Irene had hands of gold and should have been rich but she just wasn't a businesswoman.

After Louise graduated eighth grade she went to the one-year commercial high school on the very top floor of St. Anthony's School. I was up there once and saw typewriters with blank keys and a poster of the keyboard hung over the blackboard in the front of the room. The course was called "touch-typing" and if you could learn that and shorthand, you could get a job until somebody married you.

But Louise didn't finish and she never got a job before somebody married her. She was too good-looking to touch-type and it wasn't long before she was pregnant, having tempted the wrong man or maybe the right man since he married her and got them Jimmy Radiccio's old apartment across the hall from her mother. I'd see Louise with her baby, as regal as ever, her pants sewed on so they'd be as tight as you could get them, and her eyes rimmed in black liquid from a pen she didn't have to steal from her sisters anymore.

Later I heard that her husband was "connected" and that she had three more kids and lived in a big house in New Jersey with a fountain in the entrance hall. I moved away but whenever I came back, my mother would fill me in. Louise's husband had gone to jail and Louise was back in the tenement on Thompson Street, in 194, living with her mother.

My mother said it was a lesson. Louise wasn't the first girl to marry a wiseguy as a way up only to end down. Vera next door had done just that and when her husband was taken away in a straitjacket to Bellevue one night with the whole building outside watching, she was left with three kids and a pity check from the Mob and had to go work in Sutter's Bakery on Greenwich Avenue.

"How do you know?" I said to my mother. "That she didn't marry for love?" But I was just being provocative. I knew that in the neighborhood you married for love if nothing better came along. You only had one chance.

But Louise beat the odds. She found another husband, word on the street a nice guy, and she got another house. Bigger, this time, with the fountains on the outside. I wasn't surprised. Louise was never afraid; she was what we called "stand-up." And when I went to church with my mother on a visit home, and sat behind old Sister Pauline, still terrifying the children at the nine o'clock Mass, I thought, "So there!"

THE MÉNAGE

I didn't know Rosie then, when she lived on the beach in Calangute with her old man and the English couple. I could see her from my house when she would come out in the mornings to sweep. They were all four of them tall and beautiful, I remember, both the English girl and Rosie with wild red hair. They kept to themselves and I wasn't interested in new friends. I was too busy licking my wounds.

There were whispers about them, about what was going on in that house, but for me, it was all a scandal. You could find me on the beach in a dress, a black dress, if you can believe it, among the naked and the loinclothed. It takes time to take off your clothes when you were raised by Irish nuns in a country founded by Puritans.

One morning I saw Rosie's old man leave. I could tell he was leaving because he was wearing clothes. He had a rucksack over one shoulder and he was walking toward the road, sinking to his ankles in the soft sand with every step. And then there were three. The Englishman and his redheads in that house on the beach.

• • •

Calangute was the first beach you hit in Goa when you came in from Panjim. You thought you were in paradise at first: white sand and swaying palms, everyone young and tanned and undressed, whitewashed houses with an ocean view for a few rupiahs, chillums firing on every porch, sunset parties with *Abbey Road* playing over and over on a tape deck until the batteries ran out. The local priest delivered *ganga* on his bicycle and the coconuts fell off the trees.

But rumors were rife. Was it the French chef from Grenoble who stole cameras from the Swedes to buy a goat to roast on a spit for his birthday? Had the Dutch girl really sold her baby to Father Damien who brought it to the nuns in Cochin? Was it true that religious pilgrims had bitten off several toes from the body of St. Francis Xavier in the Basilica of Bom Jesus in Old Goa?

The stories traveled on air, they appeared in mangoes, they wrapped themselves in sarongs and I took them in, swaying in my hammock on my porch overlooking the sea, but mostly I obsessed about Rosie and the English couple, watching Rosie bend over in front of her house with a broom of twigs and then step into the darkness of the open doorway.

I stayed around for a while, until neighbors stole my clothes and men got tiresome. Claus was indifferent and Achilles gave me a sexually transmitted disease. I was done with the East.

The day I left, the ménage were sitting cross-legged in a circle eating lychees. It was the season. I had never seen them all three together in one place and I stood a long while watching as they pulled the fruit from the branches and peeled off the rough pink-brown rind. The Englishman fed the redheads the slippery white flesh with his fingers; Rosie fed the English girl and the English girl fed Rosie. The English girl stood and the

Englishman reached up and held her arm but she pulled away and disappeared into the grove of palm trees behind the house. Rosie and the Englishman got up and went inside, one following the other.

It was none of my business what was going on but I did think about walking over and looking in through the slot of the window, squinting into the cool dark of that white stucco house, but I didn't. Instead I took what hadn't been stolen and caught a *becak* to the bus station.

So there I was in Australia, in Sydney, working in a pub that recreated the Tyrolean Alps. I wore an appropriately humiliating costume and pink suede clogs and one Friday night came home to find Rosie holding court in the living room of the house I shared with three expat Pommies and a local actress.

More stunning than I remembered, an Indonesian batik sarong tight on her hips, Rosie told stories. She nodded to me when I came into the room and ignored me when I walked out.

She found me later and we hit it off, Rosie and I, and we left together for Bali on Garuda Airlines. It wasn't until weeks later that I told her I had been in Goa.

"Really?" she said. "When?"

We were lying side by side on rope beds in a shack on Kuta Beach.

"Not sure exactly. A year ago? Two?"

"Ah, yeah," she said, and rolled on her side and started picking at the mold that was growing on the leather bag she had carried from Sydney.

"Nice, that, Goa," she said. "Christ, it's good to be out of Aussie."

"You were living in a house on the beach . . . in Calangute."

"Right. Then it got fucked. All those junkies. Everyone started moving to Anjuna." She turned back to face me. "What were you doing there, darling?" she said.

"Nursing a broken heart."

"Oh, that." She laughed.

"You don't remember me at all?"

"Not likely. Not much in common. This heart of mine doesn't break."

I suspected as much, which is why I had left Sydney with her. I thought I could learn something.

"Goa," she said. "Ian and Cynthia." Her voice was low and sultry. "That was a story."

"Tell me," I said, and when she started to talk I lay back and closed my eyes.

They had met on the beach, Cynthia and Ian and Rosie and John. They had all just arrived when Father Damien stopped his bicycle and asked if they were looking to rent a house. Ian said yes straightaway and they followed the priest as he walked his bicycle along the sand. They were ill-matched couples in many ways but they had a common language and the joke that both Rosie and Cynthia had that wild red hair.

"John wasn't so happy with the set-up," Rosie was saying. "He thought Ian was a bit of a bully, and you know, he was. He was big, threatening even, and he just took over."

"So John wanted to leave?"

"He did, after a while. At first we swapped partners, then we really got into it and John started getting bummed because it always ended up all about Ian. John would walk in with a newspaper cone of mandarins and find me and Cynthia and Ian all tangled up and Ian would say, 'C'mon, mate, join the party,' and in the beginning John tried but it wasn't his thing.

Complicated, foursomes are. Me, I was just having a good time. I liked John well enough but John was straight. He'd been to university. He was taking some time off to see the world, but me and Cynthia and Ian, we had nothing else going on."

I could have told her then that I had watched John leave, that I had seen Ian feeding his redheads lychees from his fingers. I could have told her that I was in the John camp. I didn't know the Ians and Rosies and Cynthias of the world, with their fearlessness, their disregard for consequences. They both attracted and repelled me.

There were a lot of them moving around in those days, shoulder to shoulder with the seekers and the students taking a break. There was opportunity for stealing and fleecing and most of all, smuggling, to feed a dream of easy money, to finance a life on the bum. There was duplicity and desperation and stupidity.

"And John left, just like that?" I said. Rosie took a long, deep toke on the joint she had rolled.

"Not that easy. He got me alone and said something like: 'What in fuck's name are you doing? Let's get out of here, away from this freak.'

"But I told him to fuck off. That Goa was a blast. The beach, the dope . . . it was one big blast. He came at me, pushed me down, started kissing me, talking in my ear, and then Ian comes in and moves right in between us. 'Groovy,' Ian says, taking my hand, putting it against his hard-on, moving his body against John. The next thing I know, the two of them are rolling around on the floor. John took the worst of it. Ian punched him bloody. John got up, packed his gear, and didn't even look back at me when he walked out."

"What happened to him?" I said. Rosie made a face.

"Fuck if I know," she said.

"So it was the two of you and Cynthia?" I said, taking the joint from her, rolling onto my back. It was so hot I could barely move. We were waiting for the rains.

"Right. Ian said it was all about me but Cynthia was having a hard time of it and I would hear him telling her how he loved her best but he loved me, too, and she had to love me, that we were family. The Trinity, he called us. The Trinity, and guess who sat at the top of the fucking triangle?"

"So what happened?"

"What always happens. We ran out of money. If John were there, he could have wired his mum and dad, but any of us? Forget it. Ian hadn't spoken to his in years, didn't even know if they were alive. Cynthia's had cut her off when she left England, and mine? They might have sent some but fucked if I was going to ask."

I watched a gecko stalk a horrifyingly large spider near the ceiling. Rosie was drifting off, stoned, but I wanted to hear the rest so I poked her awake with a toe and she laughed. "Ian started freaking out," she said. "His drugs were getting expensive. We had to pay the rent on the house. Then one night Ian said something about Cynthia and I maybe getting paid for what we gave away for free. 'I'd be right there,' he told us. 'Make sure nothing happened to you. Only businessmen . . . we could hit one of the really flash hotels up in Bombay.' Cynthia clocked him right under his eye with a teacup, the kind you broke when you finished drinking the tea. 'Bugger off, you disgusting arsehole,' she said. She might have spit in his face. She followed me outside and we put our arms around each other and realized it was us against him."

Rosie was sitting up now, enjoying her own story. "But we couldn't let him go," she said. "Ian was like that. Bluebeard, we called him. The three of us got back together that night; Ian even squeezed out a few tears, begging us to forgive, telling us how much he loved us, how we were his family, how he'd figure something out. We fell asleep in a huddle and he never brought it up again."

Rosie nodded off and, this time, there was no waking her.

If it wasn't sex, Rosie explained, it was going to have to be drugs. When Ian came up with an elaborate scheme to bring hashish into England, pure Pakistani from Chitral with the gold stamp in the corner of the brick to prove it, the redheads didn't think twice. Ian had a van that he and Cynthia had driven out East. They would drive it back the way they had come, this time with dope hidden inside, crossing some of the toughest borders in the world: Pakistan, Afghanistan, Iran, Turkey, Greece, countries where drug smugglers were locked up for life, executed, disappeared.

The redheads put their faith in their old man. He wasn't like some others, who sent their birds alone, convincing them that their gender would save them. They were all together in this.

The ménage was high on the future. Bad news didn't travel. It was only the triumphant who returned flashing wads of hard currency and new clothes that told the tale.

"We made it all the way to Rome," Rosie said. "They took that van apart at every border. We thought we were buggered once or twice. We sat at the Iranian border for three days. They banged, they dismembered, they shook. They knew we had it but they couldn't find it. We knew we had an advantage. Cynthia and I were distractions. They dug Ian because he had two wives and maybe our red hair drove them around the bend. Two of us, and Cynthia with skin white like milk glass, but they still wanted to find the dope. And they had all the time in the world. But so did we."

"Where was the dope?"

"Ha! Bloody brilliant, Ian was. You had to give him that. He suspended it in glass containers inside the gas tank. Everyone stashes it in doors and panels and floorboards but they always find it when it's in the body of the car. Remember when every stall in the market was flogging false-bottom suitcases and hollow Buddhas?" Rosie shook her head. "Stupid, that was."

I didn't remember but I did want the rest of the story. I could see Rosie losing interest. She found a bag of cashews and said something about going for a swim. "And then?" I prodded. She poured cashews into my hand. They were spiced and salted and I licked my fingers and asked her again. She stretched her long freckled arms above her head.

"So we got to Rome, all the way to effing Rome and we were dead broke. Ian got out some dope to sell, just enough to get us to London. We made it all the way to Rome and ended up busted for a couple of joints."

"Jesus," I said.

"Jesus is right. We went to jail. Ian in the men's part, Cynthia and I in the women's. It was a trip, Italian jail. Nuns ran it and with a bit of lire, you could have anything you wanted. Cynthia and I plastered the walls of our cell with pages ripped out of fashion magazines. We had a standing order for chocolate and fags, English ones, Rothman's, Dunhill. We played with the babies when we got really bored. Didya know? In Italy, you keep your baby with you in jail. The women were in for smuggling cigarettes and murdering their cheating men. But the food! Spaghetti twice a day. *Nudo*, they called it, naked spaghetti. Nothing on it, not even salt. And every meal those Italian birds would smack their lips. 'Mmmm,' they'd say. 'Pasta!' Sometimes Cynthia and I would just have lollies and chips, we couldn't look at another limp string of wet noodle."

Rosie turned over on her stomach, folded her hands under her chin. "My mum and dad came up with the money for a lawyer. Poor luvs."

"You got off?"

"Cynthia and I did three months. Then, free as birds." She laughed at the pun. "Two innocent young girls drawn into crime by, what else? The sweet talk of a bad man."

"You gave Ian up?"

"You could say that."

"What happened to him?"

"In prison, for a very long time, I'm afraid. He was pissed he took the rap. Selling dope was one thing but worse was the morals charge. The judge said he corrupted us, Cynthia and I, *le innocente*. You should have seen us in court. We looked like schoolgirls. My mum sent us the sweetest flowered dresses." Rosie faced me when she said this.

"And Cynthia?"

"We kissed for the last time at the Rome airport."

"Didn't you feel bad for Ian?"

"Oh, darling, have you not learned anything?"

I should have by now, I thought. I wanted to tell Rosie I was trying, which was why I was here with her. I wasn't wearing dresses on the beach anymore.

The rains began and shook the tin roof. Water leaked along the openings near the ceiling. The gecko had caught the spider and was feasting in a corner. We would have to wait if we wanted to go for a swim.

Rosie said she had a better idea. We should find ourselves some rich blokes, she said. We shouldn't have to buy our own dope or pay for a room. Enough, she said, with these long-haired freaks. Tomorrow we should go over to that new resort, the Inna Grand. We would book a suite and lay out by the pool.

"How can we afford that?" I said.

She leaned over and kissed me on the mouth. She traced an eyebrow with a delicate finger. "Honestly, luv," she said. "What do you think happened to all that dope in the van?" Then she took me in her arms and together we listened to the rain.

THE BABY

1968

Robin and Christina had a plan to meet in Le Havre and go on to Paris. In the flea market there they would buy backpacks, or as Robin, having been to Europe before, called them, rucksacks, and they would hitchhike, or as Robin called it, autostop, across Europe. The goal was a beach where they could wait out the summer and read serious novels, or as Robin said, find an older man with a yacht who would take them to deserted islets for picnics. They would have just graduated, nubile, with degrees in English literature. "Why not?" Robin said.

They were a compatible pair: Robin being the brains, Christina the entertainment. Robin set the stage: they would wear dresses, they would not get into a car with more than one man, and they would carry their own food in a basket with two handles, one for each of them, baguettes and Camembert in France, mozzarella and tomatoes in Italy, and in Greece, watermelons as round as basketballs.

But then came the fly in the ointment, the thrown monkey wrench. When she thought back, Christina wondered how she let it happen. Her mother had warned her from the moment she bled. She was thirteen, struggling to untwist the elastic straps that held a sanitary napkin in place. "Just remember, Christina," her mother had said. "It's always your problem. Them? They just zip up their pants and walk away."

That's for sure.

Jason had shown up one night a few days after they met, high on black beauties and the gig he had just finished jumping around the stage at Hernando's Hideaway off Route 635 making like Mick Jagger. He had a cardboard box of 3 Musketeers under his arm. Christina's favorite, how did he know? Twelve candy bars in their original carton. Her roommate was out with a guy named Hans who would later hijack a plane to Cuba. Christina did not expect them home anytime soon. Still, what was she thinking?

Skinny and soft-spoken, with a halo of frizzy hair, Jason was the only son of a Long Island surgeon and a homemaker, determined to disappoint them both. What a cliché.

Christina had let him into her bed but was soon bored, black beauties will do that, she knew, and when she finally got rid of him, she had an uneasy feeling that something momentous had happened. She ate the candy bars, one after the other, making a neat pile of the wrappers that she smoothed flat with the side of her hand, remembering her Uncle John who would iron his bankroll, one single dollar at a time. Now? she thought. She had screwed up now?

The waiting began. She tried to will it out of existence. She took scalding baths. She paused at the top of every flight of stairs, imagining throwing herself down to the bottom. She prayed. Didn't God take mercy on sinners? Was she a sinner? She agreed to cop to the sin if it involved mercy. She had been called an occasion of sin, in the dark of the confessional box when she was thirteen. Had she become a self-fulfilling prophecy?

Christina told Robin, and only Robin. If Christina had told her father, he would have been silent and dismissive. Her mother would have tearily taken her in her arms, with an offer to raise the baby while Christina languished in a local dead-end job, like cashier at the five-and-dime store on Sixth Avenue. The job would be provided by the neighborhood wiseguys who fenced stolen goods and played cards in the café with the blackened windows. It would have been a favor to her family. Where Christina came from, they took care of their own.

Robin came right over when Christina called. "How the hell did this happen?" she said.

"Oh, please. You're kidding me, right?"

"Well, now what?"

"I don't know. Isn't that why you're here? So we can figure something out?"

"This has been happening a lot this year, like some kind of virus," Robin said. She looked as though she were thinking hard. "There was Lydia, and Marilyn and Susan and . . ."

Christina sighed. "It's no revelation, Robin. This has been happening since the Garden of Eden."

"The Garden of Eden?"

"Yeah. Adam was high and Eve was a moron, seduced by a box of cheap candy bars. Can you concentrate please? What am I going to do?"

"Do you want it?"

"No, I don't want it . . . I don't want any part of it. I want it to go away. I want it to not be."

"OK," Robin said. "Options."

"I'm waiting."

"Go someplace. Have the baby. Give it away."

"The Saint Maria Goretti Home for Unwed Mothers run by the Sisters of Endless Charity? No, thank you." Christina took a drag of her cigarette. She blew the smoke up into her nostrils and out her mouth. It was an act she had spent time perfecting. It made her feel tough and in control. "What did that girl on the fourth floor do? The one who thought she was getting fat?"

"Lydia. She went to Pennsylvania," Robin said, opening her hands in supplication. "Should we go talk to her?"

"No."

"Why not?"

"I'm not going to some defrocked alcoholic quack in rural Pennsylvania."

"You've seen too many movies," Robin said. "Marilyn. What did Marilyn do?"

"She miscarried after that the drummer in her boyfriend's band found a midwife from the Fifth Ward to stick a rubber tube in her uterus."

"Your boyfriend's in a band."

"He's not my boyfriend and no one in his band knows anyone in the Fifth Ward. And I'm not bleeding out in a motel room on South Salina Street."

Robin understood. The alternatives were grim. She had her own ideas but kept them to herself. The nuns at her fancy private convent school in Boston had been liberal but they were sticklers for the sanctity of life. "We're not making any progress," she said finally.

"Shit. I can't believe this. How stupid. How goddamn stupid."

"It could still be a false alarm." But Christina knew different. She didn't need a dead rabbit to tell her she was pregnant.

Life went on, as it does. Christina took exams and handed in papers. She checked her underpants for a red stain. She imagined cramps. She kept praying, cutting deals with random saints. She avoided the Blessed Mother, who she didn't think would be on her side.

Christina remembered a joke where a woman goes to the doctor and when he tells her she's pregnant, the woman insists she's a virgin, after which the doctor takes a pair of binoculars and looks out the window. "What are you doing?" the woman says. "The last time this happened," the doctor says, "three wise men came from the East."

Robin came by every day. "Anything?" she'd say.

"Nothing."

Then, eventually, "Did you tell Jason?"

"Yes."

"Well, what did he say?"

"'Marry me. I love you. It's OK you're not Jewish. We'll live on Long Island in my parents' basement and I'll go to medical school after all.'" Christina took a breath. "He said nothing."

"Nothing? Not, what are we going to do? Not, what can I do? Not, what do you need me to do? Not, do you need money?"

"Nope. He just asked if I wanted to come hear him sing Friday night at Hernando's. He said he'd get me in for free."

"I don't believe it."

"That's because you don't have a mother. If you did, you would have known. She would have told you what to expect."

"Seriously. Does being with child make you mean?"

"I'm sorry. But you want to know the truth? I'm glad he's out of the equation. He's an idiot. He'd just get in the way.

"Of what?"

"Of what I have to do."

"Which is?"

"I don't know yet. Well, I do know. I just don't know how. What are you supposed to do with a coat hanger anyway?"

"Not funny."

"Sorry."

Christina graduated. She walked with the School of Architecture because she got lost in the crowd of caps and gowns and couldn't find her place. At a party that night she saw her friend Susan, who told Christina that she had saved her a seat and where had she been?

Susan was the only other girl in the Forestry School, the only other girl stumpy. She and Christina had met the first day in a land-surveying class. Susan was at the party with her boyfriend, big blond handsome Joe, football player and summa cum laude, engineering. Christina and Susan sat in a corner and Susan told Christina that she was getting married. She showed Christina her ring and told her that Joe had a job offer in Philadelphia.

"Congratulations," Christina said. "That's great." Which was when Susan lowered her voice.

"I'm pregnant," she said. "I'm fucking pregnant." Christina didn't know what to say. When Susan started to cry, Christina rubbed her back. "I don't want to get married," Susan told her. "I don't want to live in fucking Philadelphia. I want to fight forest fires in California. I want to tag grizzlies in Yosemite. Shit shit shit."

Christina thought she should tell Susan that it would be OK, that she was lucky. Christina's mother would have said that Susan was lucky. The guy was marrying her, deflowered, spoiled, loose, easy, used goods . . . he was doing the right thing.

Instead Christina went to the bar and came back with two water glasses and a bottle of Seagram's Seven. She filled up the glasses and they drank until the bottle was empty. Joe was really pissed when he came to get Susan and she could hardly stand up. He was pissed at Susan and he was pissed at Christina. It made Christina realize that things could be worse.

Not long after, Christina asked Robin to come meet her in the city.

"What are we doing here?" Robin said, sitting across the table from Christina at Serendipity 3 on East Sixtieth Street.

"I was coming uptown and felt like an ice cream sundae."

"You know we leave soon."

"I know and I've got a plan."

"Tell me."

"Where are we going?"

"We're supposed to go to Greece."

"Right. And how do we get there?"

"Auto-stop through France, Italy and Yugoslavia, down to Athens and then . . ."

"Stop. Stop. We go through Belgrade, right?"

"Yeah, so?"

Christina stage-whispered, "I can get it done in Belgrade." Christina sat back. "They call it a 'termination.' It's legal. In a hospital. I got the address. Three hundred American. Cash. Walk in. Overnight stay. I just came from the embassy. Say something."

"What can I say? This is amazing."

"I know. They're legalizing it in other places in Europe but it's more complicated. The guy I spoke to at the embassy was excited to tie the availability of termination to the superiority of communism." Christina showed Robin the diplomat's card. The name and address of the clinic was written on the back.

"I guess we're set, then."

"All set. What a relief!" Christina put her hand on Robin's arm. "Thanks for this," she said. "I could never do it alone."

"Hey, it's going to be alright," Robin said. She took Christina's hand.

Christina had booked a student ship months before thinking it would be fun but it wasn't, and she spent the ten-day crossing nauseous in the top bunk of her four-person stateroom that was next to the engine feeling sad, lonely, and deserted. She was never so happy to arrive anywhere as she was when the ship docked at Le Havre and Robin was standing there with two rucksacks.

They put their arms around each other and Robin said she had bought the rucksacks in Amsterdam to save time. She had cycled down to France with them tied on her bike rack. They could leave right away, Robin told her. They could leave right then and they did, thumbing their way through France and Italy and Yugoslavia. They knew they were stopping in Belgrade but neither of them said it aloud.

Belgrade was a city they would have passed through without a second thought, but not this time. They arrived late in the day and found their way to the clinic. Robin stayed outside. The doctor was thick and leering and he took Christina into his office and sat behind his desk. He asked Christina why she was there, although he had to know. It was an abortion clinic after all. She could not say the word "abortion." It stuck in her throat like the crime she thought it was and when the leering doctor said, "You are here for a termination?" she felt so much better, such an easier word for what she was about to do.

"Yes," she said, and when he asked for the money, she took out the American dollars in twenties and handed them to him over the desk. He counted them like a banker, and satisfied, he looked up.

"So, you and your great country . . . you have come here for what you need because here we are an advanced and modern society." Christina said yes again and he told her to come back at five o'clock.

Outside, Robin was sitting on the curb, waiting. Christina sat down next to her and started crying. Robin cried with her. They held each other, two American girls in summer dresses with WWII rucksacks next to them on the sidewalk, sobbing. No one gave them a second look.

Robin was the first to stop crying. She was, after all, the brains. "You don't have to do it," she said. "You can have the baby. We'll go somewhere, someplace in Europe. We can raise the baby together. We can do this." Christina stopped crying. She looked up. "Let's go," Robin said. "If we leave now, we can get out of this shitty town before it gets dark. We can get back on the road." And they left, right then and there. They hoisted their rucksacks and walked to the road. Christina sat on a rock while Robin stood out front and held out her hand, thumb raised. Destination: Greece. They don't talk about the pregnancy anymore. They don't talk about the baby.

1988

Christina was in Huntington Hartford's duplex on Beekman Place. She had come with her new boyfriend who owned a bar on Lafayette Street. He was a hybrid, like Christina. He grew up rough but studied art in Florence and was a painter until he took a job at Max's Kansas City and then opened his own bar where artists held him in bear hugs and kissed him on both cheeks, pretending they were tough guys. Christina's boyfriend really was a tough guy. He had brought her there with his up-and-coming wiseguy friends with names like Richie One and Richie Two who somehow latched onto Huntington Hartford, who was by then old and sad and debauched and not careful about his friends. But he still had this very beautiful duplex on Beekman Place where he invited people like Richie One and Richie Two to join in the debauchery.

Christina was wandering around the many rooms and she found the man himself, alone on a sofa, high on drugs, and he patted the cushion next to him and told her to come sit down. She suspected that, in the next room, Richie One and Richie Two were rolling up the oriental rugs and flinging first editions out of the bookshelves just for fun.

She sat down and Huntington Hartford took her hand in his. He was an old man and Christina felt sorry for him but what could she do? And then he leaned close to her and said, "Tell me a secret."

"A secret?"

"Yes, please."

"OK," she said.

"Good," he said, "begin," and he put his head back against the sofa and closed his eyes.

"I was in Greece," Christina began. "And I was pregnant with this baby that I never wanted but I was going to have it anyway. I was going to have it and raise it somewhere in Europe with my friend Robin. She had convinced me we could do it. She was the brains, you see."

"And you?" he interrupted.

Christina laughed. "I was the entertainment."

"Go on."

"The baby was a secret. No one but Robin and I knew about it. I was going to have an abortion in Belgrade but in the end I couldn't do it."

Christina thought he wasn't listening, that he might have fallen asleep or nodded off, but then he said, "Belgrade?"

"Not important."

"And the father?"

"Not important either."

"I understand. And this Robin?"

"She was my best friend."

"You were lovers?"

Christina poked him in the ribs. "You only get one secret," she said.

"Sorry," he told her. "I've always been a greedy bastard. Then what?"

"We decided I would have the baby in Italy, near where my mother is from. It was a dumb idea. Two American girls, in sundresses, in a southern Italian village, one with a *la banza* out to here, not a man in sight and Robin with the face of a Madonna, this perfectly oval face, blue eyes . . . the men would salivate like werewolves at the full moon."

Huntington Hartford sat up. "Pity," he said. "If I had known you then, I would have helped." Christina believed him. She understood that he had never wanted anything he couldn't have. He had built an art museum, for Christ's sake, which was really all she knew about him. "Go on," he said, settling back.

"We were two Catholic girls. We found a convent, way in the country, outside of Matera. I had the baby, a boy, and I let the sisters name him. They were so excited. They called him Bruno after the Madonna della Bruna. And they passed him around until he screamed for mercy. They said we could stay. We could raise Bruno there and they would help us.

"But the next morning, we left. We didn't talk about it, Robin and I. We just got up in the morning, packed our rucksacks and walked out. We didn't say goodbye to the sisters. We stuffed the doorbell so it wouldn't ring when we opened the gate. I had just had a baby and I bled and bled for days. Robin asked if I wanted to stop but I said, 'No. Let's keep going.'"

Huntington Hartford was quiet. Christina could hear crashing noises outside the room and thought she should say something. She stood up but he took her arm and told her to sit. "It doesn't matter," he said. "But tell me, this is really a secret?"

"I swear to God," Christina said, and the both of them laughed. "You are the first person I have ever told. I haven't thought about it until now, not ever. Robin and I separated a few months later and haven't spoken since. The last I heard she was living in California."

He patted her arm, closed his eyes, and fell asleep. There was a whistle in his throat when he breathed. Christina left the apartment on her own. Richie One and Richie Two were burning books in the fireplace.

That night, she dug out an old address book, the ink faded. She found the last number she had for Robin and dialed it. Robin picked up on the third ring but Christina didn't speak.

"Hello? Who is it? Hello?"

"Robin. It's Christina."

"My God, Christina." It was all she said.

"Robin, you remember that summer we went to Europe . . ."

"Of course."

"The summer I was pregnant?"

"Yes."

"I've been thinking about the baby. What might have happened to him. Where he might be now. I was thinking we could go back. We could try to find him. Wouldn't that be something? To go back and find him? Would you do that with me?"

Silence.

"Christina, what baby?"

"You just said you remembered. The baby, the baby I had in Italy that we left with the sisters in the convent outside Matera. The baby I had that summer."

"Christina, you never had the baby. We went to the clinic in Belgrade, remember? You had the abortion in Belgrade and then we went to Greece. I picked you up the next morning and we left."

Silence.

"Christina?"

"Yes, I do remember. We left the next morning for Greece and I bled and bled. I bled for days."

DEATH BECOMES HER

Madam Life's a piece in bloom
Death goes dogging everywhere:
She's the tenant of the room,
He's the ruffian on the stair.
—William Ernest Henley

My mother is dying in her bed across the street. My husband is in the hospital, defying the medical prediction that he had six months to live. It's been ten and we're still counting. Me, I'm going back and forth from the hospital to my mother's bedside to my job at a celebrity fashion magazine. Is Nicole Kidman wearing Zac Posen, and did she really buy her lasagna pan at Williams-Sonoma? Can you fax that information, please? It's a very high-end magazine and we care about the veracity of what we print.

Today my husband wants knishes from Yonah Schimmel and chicken noodle soup from the Second Avenue deli. I bring these things and watch him eat them. It's a very high-end hospital, but coming from the outside, from the clear cold of fall, it smells bad. I'm grateful for working at a very high-end magazine and not in a hospital. I'm grateful for a lot these days. I bring my husband things that I hope will make him as happy as he can be in a hospital on borrowed time. The aides like him. They are all praying, he tells me, and asks for twenty-dollar bills to hand out, which he has always liked doing. I don't know what to talk about, so I clean things, although I hate it. He has always been so fastidious in his personal habits that I know it's hard for him in here. At home, too weak to stand at the sink to perform his ablutions, always extensive and done in private, he pulls a chair into the bathroom and soldiers on.

I go in to see my mother. Only a week ago, I came from work to find them both, my husband and my mother, in her bedroom. He had found her on the floor, gotten her back into bed. "I had a feeling about her today," he told me. "I came back to see her. I was here this afternoon and I had a feeling."

I stayed with my mother that night and went home at six in the morning. My husband said something was wrong and I took him to the hospital. I left for the magazine and Cameron Diaz's shoes and did you know she doesn't have such great skin?

I held my mother's hand and smoothed her brow. She couldn't talk, but I knew she could hear. I had never cleared up in my mind how I felt about the afterlife. There's a lot of ritual around death in Italian American culture. Our local funeral parlors, which numbered three in a two-block radius, are now down to one, but our undertaker, Peter DeLuca, knows how to do it right. He visits the senior citizens' center in the basement of the church to assure the ancient ones that he knows how to do it right.

I'm clear on the fact that my mother wants to wear a short dress (not one of those tulle gowns they sell you last minute in the funeral parlor) and have a fully open coffin—she wants her legs to show. She's always had good legs. (Half-open coffins are cheaper, and you don't have to wear stockings and shoes.) She's had her outfit picked out for years. So many years, in fact, that the chosen dress went out of style and we had to start all over again. She decided on the dress she wore to her only grandson's wedding, the grandson she insists she doesn't favor, but the five granddaughters know better. My mother has always favored boys. Did I mention I have a brother?

Beige satin dress, lace at the bodice, matching shoes, all put away in tissue paper. She has told me where everything is at least once a week, whenever the conversation turns to who has died (often) and what the corpse was wearing at the last wake she went to (also often). For music, she wants "Ave Maria" and "Amazing Grace" (that Protestant song that was let into the Catholic canon I'm not sure when).

But what about the afterlife? All I had was this vague Buddhist/animist/humanist idea that I'd cobbled together, once I'd "left" the church after a priest in the confessional told my fourteen-year-old self that kissing with your mouth open was a mortal sin.

Now my mother, this woman I've loved my whole life, is leaving me. To go where? Heaven? Might all those St. Peter jokes about the pearly gates be true?

St. Peter greets you at the gate and invites you in for dinner. He serves you tea and toast. Wait a minute, you say. Tea and toast? This is heaven?

I know, St. Peter says, but it just doesn't pay to cook for two . . .

I hold her hand and I have a vision. There's the porcelain table set in cement under the grape arbor at my grandparents' house on Long Island. Everyone is there—my father, my mother's three sisters. It's summer and there's a breeze; it's cool under the grape arbor. My mother's sisters are all in flowered housedresses, and my Aunt Rae is coming out of the house, kicking open the screen door with her foot because in her arms she's carrying a huge bowl of spaghetti, spaghetti with gravy, sausage, and meatballs made with pignoli and raisins. I lean over my mother and I tell her what I see. "They're waiting for you," I tell her. "They are all there waiting for you. They won't start eating without you."

And I'm convinced. I know that this is where she's going, back to the people she's loved and lost, back to the good times. And I tell her that if she wants, my father will come get her, pick her up in the roadster, and she can be fifteen again and wear the coat he bought her to wear when she met his family, the green wool coat with the fox collar, and the cloche hat.

But she won't go. She won't leave. My brother is in Europe. She's not leaving, I realize, without saying goodbye to her son. The others will have to wait.

I go to see my husband in the hospital every day. I leave work early. The doctor says he has to stay until a certain something happens. I can't stand the hospital. I can't stand the smell. I can't stand the table on wheels that goes over the bed, and the IV dangling and the hospital gowns that I sneak into the closet and take out when no one is looking, also blankets and other things, so that he can have them changed constantly, because . . . did I tell you how fastidious my husband is?

There's a crisis, and they rush him into surgery and then to the intensive care unit. The nurse asks me if he has a living will, a DNR, and tells me that I should go and get it. She says I should tell my children to come. I am surprised when she says this, but I listen. We can see him fifteen minutes every hour. The waiting room has a Coke machine. There are other families there. There are people wailing in the halls, and every time we go inside for our fifteen minutes, we see another empty bed.

My mother is dying. My husband is dying. That might be Armani that Nicole Kidman is wearing. There's no more Coke in the machine. My husband opens his eyes and decides not to die just then.

My brother comes home. I tell him to let our mother go. He says he can't, and he sits with her for a day and a night. He sits in the chair in the living room, where he always sits when he comes to see her. In the morning, he lets her go—to Long Island, to eat spaghetti under the grape arbor with her husband and her sisters.

I take the dress and the shoes out of the closet. She needs underwear. I buy her a $200 pink lace bra and matching underpants. My husband would tease her that one day Peter DeLuca would see her in her underwear. My brother and I go to the funeral home to see Peter DeLuca, and we take the elevator to the basement to look at coffins. We are having a good time. We pick out a beautiful, solid mahogany coffin with brass hardware. It's so beautiful, I want one for myself.

My mother is old. She's lived in this neighborhood her whole life. The dream in this neighborhood is to have many people at your wake and many flowers. It's a sign you were beloved, cherished, respected. I worry that she has lived too old for all of this. Who's left to fill the funeral parlor with flowers? Who will come to show she's beloved?

The funeral parlor has two rooms: a front room and a back room. One is bigger than the other. Not everyone needs a big room. Not everyone is beloved, cherished, respected.

My mother's wake takes over the whole funeral parlor. We are lucky, Peter tell us, that no one else has died this week, because we need both rooms, the front and the back. There are flowers everywhere. There are people everywhere. All afternoon and all night for two days they come and go. My mother is having a wake to beat the band. She was almost ninety years old. She is wearing her beautiful dress and her $200 bra and matching underpants, and her lovely legs and satin shoes are showing beneath the chiffon hem of her dress . . . and the coffin. Did I tell you the coffin was so beautiful that I wanted one for myself?

I dig out all of my beautiful black clothes. Cashmere pants and high-heeled boots; uneven-hemmed skirts and blouses with illusion net for sleeves. I line my eyes and paint my mouth for the funeral Mass. I walk up the church aisle and give a eulogy. I say my mother always believed that everyone loved her, and after this I believe it, too.

And we go in limousines to Calvary Cemetery, to the grave my father had bought many years before he needed it. There's room for six bodies in there, and the double granite headstone has our family name carved into the top in bold letters. My mother talked about the grave, too. She wanted to go side by side with my father. Don't forget, she would always tell me, side-by-side.

I'm high after the funeral. The good death, the perfect wake, the perfect funeral, but it isn't over for me yet. My husband loved my mother. He saw her every day. He talked about not knowing what he would do when she wasn't there anymore, when he couldn't stop by her house, any time of the day, to eat a banana, to take a hard candy, a glass of water, use the bathroom. She lived on the ground floor. Everyone in the family had a key, ten of us. Ten people could open her door with their own key and take a banana from the fruit bowl on her counter.

Now she had died and he couldn't even go to her funeral. I don't remember if this upset him, or if he was too preoccupied with his own struggle. I don't remember talking to him about her dying, about my vision. To be honest, I don't really remember the smell of the hospital or exactly what I did there. Not even like childbirth. I can tell you the story about childbirth, but I can't tell you much about this. I don't even know if the facts are straight, the sequence of events. It's confused. I just got myself from place to place.

My husband wanted to come home. I called the doctor, who told me I was negative and unhelpful, and that we had to make a decision to keep trying or to go into hospice. My husband came home. He said he wanted to try whatever they were promising. We made an appointment to go back to see the doctor in his office. The doctor who had said six months was now trying. My husband had bought him lavender socks when he had laughed at my husband's pink ones.

Every week in that doctor's waiting room, people disappeared. My husband and I would joke about how long the guy at the end of the couch had left. We'd elbow each other at the signs we had learned meant someone was on the way out. The color, the bloat, the walk. Do I look that bad? my husband would say, and I would say no, you look good. You look like you will live forever.

I cut a small cartoon out of the *Wall Street Journal*. It was a little grim reaper, his robe dragging on the floor. He was standing on a stoop, and a man was opening the door, and the line was: "Somehow I though you'd be taller." I wanted my husband to welcome death, to stop struggling, to stop suffering, but I couldn't put myself in his shoes. I was healthy and very much alive. I was one to talk.

The day of trying came, and my husband said he couldn't. He could not get up and get dressed (fastidiously, you'll remember), and go down those many flights of steps that are our apartment and into the street and into that office, and be the guy on the end of the couch. I wanted to try, he said, for you, for the kids, but I just can't.

I called hospice and the dying went into full gear. It's wonderful, the attention you get when you're dying, the attention you cannot have when your life is still open-ended. Suddenly, there are all these people who care about you, your comfort, your well-being. They love you. They travel great distances to see you, they bring you presents, they let you talk, they stay late, they want to be near you.

We always worried about all those stairs, my husband and I. What would happen when we got old, when we got sick, broke a leg, a hip? Stairs . . . stairs . . .

And in the end, it was about the stairs. It was the stairs that made my husband decide to stop trying. The stairs decided for him. I love those stairs and I'm not afraid of them anymore. I even imagine living out my life on the top floor, never going out because of the stairs, like a mad old woman in the attic.

My husband lived six weeks. I bought him cashmere sweaters and fur-lined slippers. The nurse came, the doctor came, the priest came, the minister came, the social worker came, his brother and sister came. Ariane and Ruby and Lucy came to stay. Lucy brought him a cat that he said he didn't want, but lay with day after day and called "my buddy." Genny came, and Gianni and Matteo and Sara and Leo. Kate came. She brought cat toys.

We drank Moët & Chandon and ate Iranian caviar with hard-boiled eggs. We ate trays of lasagna and artichokes as big as a baby's head, stuffed with egg and bread crumbs and parmigiano cheese.

Thanksgiving morning, my husband couldn't get up and he stayed in bed. I said something about Christmas to the hospice nurse who came every day, and she said he wouldn't be there at Christmas. She said it wouldn't be long. She said it was close, but I didn't see it. Can you see death coming? We sat around the bed, all of us women and that cat. We gave my husband morphine with an eyedropper, and ice chips laced with vodka.

I slept next to him, and in the morning I was stunned that he was still alive, warm and lying next to me. I was amazed that he had survived the night, but I knew he was very close to Hades. He might already be on that boat. Did he have the fare?

We gathered around the bed, all of us women and that cat.

When I was a little girl, living in a tenement down the street, a neighbor came to the door to ask my mother to come upstairs, because the woman's mother had just died. My mother took me with her, rather than leaving me behind alone. Have I told you how much I loved my mother? We went upstairs and my mother closed the dead woman's eyes. I still remember the gesture: she used two fingers, her index and third on her right hand, and closed the woman's eyes. Then she took a white handkerchief and tied it around the old woman's head, to keep her mouth closed so it wouldn't freeze in an open position, because your mouth goes slack when you die. I learned that standing next to my mother. I remember the old woman in the bed, propped up against the pillows, looking like a cartoon character with a toothache.

There was the death rattle. It is a rattle and it lasts a long time. When it stopped, I lay against my husband's body. I could feel him going cold. I had promised him I would wash him. I had promised to have him wrapped in a sheet. I had promised that he would not have a wake, that he would not be carelessly dressed (have I told you how fastidious my husband was?), that he would be in a plain pine box, and that he would be cremated.

I promised that if I married a hundred times more, it would be his ashes that would be put in my coffin.

I called the undertaker and I realized that undertakers come when you call. You don't have to wait until morning or leave a message. Someone always answers. The undertaker always comes. Things move smoothly around death.

They took the body, carried it down all those stairs. We huddled, the girls and I, in another room. We did not want to see this indignity, his body being removed and carried down the stairs. I think they used a stretcher. I remember my mother telling how they took my grandfather's body down the stairs in a basket. How does a body fit in a basket?

My husband is dead and I am a widow, the survivor, the star. But there won't be a wake. I cannot be the star. I cannot dress carefully in black and sit in the big chair in the front row of the big room in the funeral parlor and clutch a linen handkerchief with which to wipe my tears. Did I tell you my husband didn't want a wake?

There was a Mass, and again I carefully chose my black clothes and did my hair and painted my mouth and lined my eyes in black. I read the eulogy from the pulpit, in the same spot where I had stood only six weeks before. I didn't cry. I didn't falter. I was elegant. I felt beautiful and powerful and very much alive. Outside, the world was Technicolor. Everything I touched felt electric.

I have a vision. My mother is at the stove; my husband is at the kitchen table. The sun is coming in the window. She is cooking for him.

A SMUGGLING CASE

Veronica sits, a grand juror, reluctant. She's lost her income for fifteen months. The prosecutor presents the first case, a smuggling case: bringing heroin and cocaine illegally into the United States.

Her fellow jurors are an easygoing bunch, happy to get the subway fare and the forty-dollars-a-day stipend. The non-easygoing are a combination of obsequious, annoying, and pretentious. No one is attractive but she does like the woman who has named her sons after Al Pacino movie characters, except for the eldest, whose first name is Alpachino. She explains carefully that she has spelled it differently. This is something to write home about.

Veronica thinks about drugs. Veronica is so respectable now. Sometimes she will smoke a joint on the street with her friend who owns a hair salon. She will get her hair done and then they will go out to eat and drink, but first they will smoke a joint that has been smoked before and stashed in a jeweled makeup case. She likes the feeling of being high. She says as they walk down the street, "I am so stoned," and worries she will never come down.

Sometimes Veronica imagines she will get arrested and show up in night court in handcuffs, which would be embarrassing.

Her youngest daughter is a prosecutor and has warned her about getting arrested. But she's sure it's only a misdemeanor despite Rockefeller and his drug laws, which she thinks might have been repealed.

In college Veronica and her friends were so paranoid they would spend half the night looking for a place to hide the marijuana. "Here, quick! Inside the pillowcase," someone would say.

"Great idea! The pillowcase."

"How about the dresser drawer? In the back, behind the socks?"

"Yes, yes! Good idea."

They shuddered at the thought of a knock on the door and turned up Simon and Garfunkel on the stereo.

Then there was the time the *federales* raided the beach huts in Acapulco. Veronica was lucky that time, she and her English boyfriend who would end up a junkie in India fixing with works he rented from pharmacies for ten paise. They had watched as the cereal boxes were emptied, their clothes strewn around. But they were clean that night and stood dumbly by as the others were taken away. It was like that. You felt bad for a while, you sat around stoned and talked about doing something to help but then you moved on, never knowing what happened to that girl who walked off the bus in the middle of the Hindu Kush or that guy who got pulled out of line at the Pakistani border. There was nothing to do but move on.

And what about when Veronica was going through Central America and she got a ride at the Guatemalan border in a truck going all the way to Nicaragua with supplies for the earthquake victims? The driver, Manuel, was sweaty, with a rice gut, a black mustache, and a cheap straw cowboy hat. The American with him, long-haired, grubby, and postulating, the type of guy who shows up in horror movies and signals bad things to come, had joined up with Manuel in Oaxaca, he said.

"I've got cocaine," he told Veronica that night.

"OK," she had said, until he told her that he had stuck it up his ass when he crossed the border from Mexico. He showed her a small plastic bag, twisted into a rope and brown from being up his ass.

"It's the best cocaine you'll ever have," he had told her but she took a pass.

Veronica is dozing but she startles herself awake when an FBI agent comes in to testify. The agent is a small, delicate Hispanic woman in a long gypsy skirt. She has a lisp. She tells the jurors about small planes bringing the drugs from Columbia, four hundred kilos at a time. The cartel is building airstrips in the jungle, she says, long enough for a plane to lift off with heavy cargo. Veronica believes her because she assumes the agent speaks Spanish and has understood the conversations over the wiretap. She trusts her and wonders if she is an FBI agent for the excitement or because it's a solid government job. But Veronica knows it's not like TV. She once met a man who joined the CIA anticipating thrills and spills but sat in a cubicle translating Russian documents about farm machinery.

Veronica listens but not so carefully. She is intrigued by this woman but it is more fun when the agent is a man. The two young girls sitting next to her, both nurses who have become friends, feel the same way. They bat their big blue eyes as a muscular, tattooed DEA agent takes the oath and looks up at the jury. Sotto voce, Alpachino's mother says, "Damn, he's married," when she spots the ring on his left hand and all the ladies laugh.

Alpachino's mother passes around a family-size bag of Doritos. She says she got them cheap in Duane Reade and that she doesn't have enough money for lunch, which is why she bought such a big bag. I think I should get involved but, like all those times on the road, I just move on.

Small planes and South America. Veronica remembers a story a pilot told her in Miami about flying single-engine prop planes into the Amazon and back for cash money, no questions asked.

"We never knew what we were carrying," he told Veronica. "And sometimes the cargo was too heavy for the plane. I knew a guy, the plane just broke in two and fell out of the sky. They told him he was carrying lobsters."

A likely story, was what Veronica thought.

The federal prosecutor presents another case after lunch. A drug mule on his way to Houston with four kilos of heroin taped to his body. The government has tapped phone calls of men with several names talking about the drugs arriving.

"Did the drug mule make it?" The jury wants to know, even though it has nothing to do with the case. Joe, the retired jazz musician who volunteered to take attendance and has told everyone about his wife and how he lived in a rented room for five years after she left because she took everything, even his clothes, scolds the jurors.

"It ain't relevant," he says, and everyone shuts up except for the three gray-haired women Veronica thinks of as the Channel 13 tote bag ladies. They always have irrelevant questions and they take many notes on small strips of paper that are supposed to go into the file at the end of the day.

• • •

Veronica remembers the worst thing she has ever done, bringing heroin into San Francisco from Bangkok. She cannot believe now that she ever did this. There were two of them, she and Rosie, who she must have loved to have gone along with such a stupid scheme. Veronica was always falling in love with women. They were few and far between on the road and they seemed like goddesses to Veronica, nothing like the women she had known at home.

She could still remember them: Heidi from Germany, a Teutonic Valkyrie, who drank Romilar for breakfast; the English Felicity in Tibetan robes, who knew where to get filet mignon in Calcutta; Australian Faye, who got Sikh cabdrivers to undo their turbans and unravel their hair so she could run her fingers through it; and of course, Rosie, the beautiful Rosie, whose whisper devoured men like the venom of a black widow spider, which suited Veronica just fine. It was always better when the men didn't hang around. Veronica had men, too, but that was different. To these women, she pledged her troth.

It was Rosie who was sleeping with Gunther who talked Rosie into taking the heroin inside her body to San Francisco.

"I have a friend in San Francisco," Gunther had told them one afternoon. "She will buy the drug from you for thousands and thousands of dollars. Easy. You will be rich. She lives in a mansion with twelve bedrooms," he went on, getting more and more excited. "And each bedroom has a slide that goes down to a secret swimming pool!"

If they had not been nipping Gunther's smack, pure and white as the newly driven snow, the story would have sounded ridiculous. It was ridiculous but they bought it anyway, Veronica and Rosie, every last word.

Veronica still wondered what Gunther had gotten out of sending them on that treacherous wild goose chase. Selling a few grams of heroin? Playing the puppeteer? Gunther was a repulsive little strung-out Kraut but Rosie always had bad taste in men. Veronica thought it was because Rosie didn't care about them, any of them, until Seth, who was lurking in San Francisco ready to undo them. Veronica couldn't even remember where they had first met Seth but she had clocked him as a hustler from the beginning, fast talking, bullshit mostly. But Rosie didn't get it. She was an Aussie and Seth to her was exotic. Veronica had forgotten how seductive a wealthy American boy who had thrown it all away could be.

After lunch, the prosecutor brings in a New York City narcotics detective. He's clean cut and handsome and he tugs at his pant legs before he sits down. He tells us about a doctor who is writing OxyContin scripts. Pills are a drug of choice today, he tells us. The numbers the detective gives us are staggering. Cars line up outside the doctor's office filled with people waiting to get prescriptions, to say they have terrible pain, but the doctor knows better. The patient arrives with cash to hand out, the detective says: $100 for the receptionist, $50 for the nurse, $250 for the doctor, who sees a new patient every ten minutes, a patient who walks out with a script for the max allowed, 180 pills, $30 each on the street. Outside, the scripts are handed over to the drivers of the cars.

Veronica and Rosie experimented with hiding the heroin in their bodies, wrapped in plastic, wrapped in condoms. Veronica remembers that Rosie was able to fit more, but it didn't matter, they were partners. They thought it would make them rich. They were so stupid. The both of them together carried less than ten grams.

The flight was long with stops in Hong Kong and Tokyo and Hawaii. Veronica remembered the koi pond in the Honolulu airport. They got to San Francisco and they put the drugs in a safe-deposit box in a bank and went to eat pastrami, which Rosie had never tasted. Then they went to find Gunther's friend who didn't exist. The street address Gunther had given them was a parking lot. Rosie said, "Let's call Seth," who invited them to stay with him. Rosie told Seth about the drugs late at night. The next day while Veronica slept, Rosie and Seth went to the bank and skipped town with the drugs.

The jury is waiting for the last case of the day. Veronica asks after Alpachino and his brothers and is upset to hear that Alpachino is in jail. His mother shrugs and says she told her son that she didn't want to know, that what he did is between him and God. The prosecutor walks in and Alpachino's mother takes her seat but not before she tells Veronica, "Every day I wake up is a new day."

The last case involves a drug dealer and a gun. The prosecutor presents and leaves the room. One of the gray-haired Channel 13 tote bag ladies is questioning the gun. It's hearsay, which is allowed in federal grand jury deliberations, but she objects. Everyone is exasperated and wants to go home. A question slows the process considerably. From the back row the subway conductor, who has told Veronica that jury duty is a lot better than driving a subway car, calls out. "If he dealing drugs, he got a gun. If he dealing drugs and he ain't got no gun, he just being stupid."

Alpachino's mother weighs in: "Gun ain't nothing special," she says. "I got friends with guns and they ain't even no drug dealers." The jurors vote and for the fourth time today, with a show of hands, the jury indicts.

We, the grand jurors, vote yes. We always vote yes. It is clear to all of us in the know that everyone is guilty.

THE CELLPHONE YOU HAVE CALLED

Teresa describes an angel carrying a fire-tipped spear with which he pierces her heart repeatedly, an act that sends her into a state of spiritual rapture. "The pain," she writes, "was so severe that it made me utter several moans. The sweetness caused by this intense pain is so extreme that one cannot possibly wish it to cease, nor is one's soul then content with anything but God."
—*The Life of Saint Teresa of Ávila by Herself*, Chapter 29

You're in a country, a restrictive one. You're alone. You're not usually alone. It's not your preferred mode of moving through the world but tomorrow you will meet colleagues. You are here to work. You've gotten off a very long flight and think about just going to bed but then you think about doing something else. There's a rooftop bar in the hotel. You tell yourself you are a grown-up; you've been one for a very long time. You can go by yourself and have a drink at the bar. You are past the age where anyone will suspect your intentions, even in a country like this. You should shower and change your clothes but instead you just go. You remember that you have certain protections in this restrictive country. You're not local and you're not young.

You get out of the elevator and stride purposefully toward the bar. You feel awkward but you keep striding. The door opens and the music is so loud you stop dead in your purposeful tracks. You decide this was not a good idea. You decide to go downstairs and get into bed. Your bravado circles down the drain of your intentions.

But when you turn to walk away, your path is blocked by two young men. They are handsome as young men are and they are well dressed. You look at them and say, "It's too loud." You don't know exactly why you are explaining yourself but since you are already acting out of character, you add, "The music." What an old fart thing to say.

But they are not put off and move, one to either side of you. "Yes, for us too," the one on your right says. "Come have a drink with us. We are going to sit outside."

Why not, you think. In truth, you do not think at all. This is something you would not do anywhere else, but you follow them, easily, happily. What you want is a drink, with company is even better. You sit with them on couches in the open air around a low table with flowers and a candle at its center. How fortuitous. How perfect.

They speak enough English. They order beers and you order a drink. They are Syrians whose families live in neighboring villages near the Lebanese border. They are here for work, as is everyone. The one across from you has a sweet face, boyish. You are curious about them; you ask them what their life is like here. They have good jobs, they say, and go home often. When they tell you their names, you forget immediately, not least because you are drinking, but also they are not names you have ever heard before. It doesn't matter. You will never see them again.

The one across from you with the sweet face tells you that he has a girlfriend, that he is in love. He wants to marry her and have children but she's Christian and his mother says no. He asks you, what should he do? You tell him he should do what he wants. You also tell him he should listen to his mother. It's not an issue you feel qualified to judge but you weigh in anyway.

The one to your right is not boyish. He is darker, heavier, sexier. He smokes. You take a cigarette from him. You hold his hand as he cups the match. He is not sympathetic about his friend's dilemma. "I'll get married when I'm forty," he says, "and one baby, girl or boy, I don't care." He stubs out his cigarette in the ashtray. He orders more drinks. He leans forward. He won't be forty for another ten years.

You laugh and tell them it is your birthday and how old you are. The sweet-faced one pretends to not believe you. The other touches your knee without commitment. "I like older women," he says. He has the blackest eyes, bedroom eyes, with long lashes. He is not boyish and his face is not sweet.

You laugh, sincerely. You don't think about what he has said, so absurd it is not even flattering. You pay the check without their noticing and get up to leave. The one with the blackest eyes puts his hand on your arm. "You cannot pay," he says. "We cannot allow that."

"I already have, habibi," you say. "It's OK."

"Then you have to have one more drink. You must let us pay. It's our custom."

You sit down and have another drink. You have no intention of not observing custom.

When you get up to leave, you are very drunk. They get into the elevator with you, your two boys. You are vaguely aware when you get out at your floor that the one with the blackest eyes has followed you.

"Let me come to your room," he says in your ear.

You are laughing. You are so very drunk. You say no because although you're no stranger to acting impulsively with men, it was more years ago than you can count, and never for such high stakes. This is a very restrictive country. In this country such things are against the law. You imagine yourself hurt, embarrassed, deported, fired, dead.

But most of all, it doesn't make any sense, which is why you are laughing. Why would this very young and handsome man want you?

"Just for a coffee. I will have a coffee and I will leave. Let me come to your room for a coffee. Please, one coffee. Please, one coffee and I will go," he says to you over and over, over and over. He says your name, over and over. It sounds very beautiful in his mouth and then, he pulls you through a door. He leans against you, pushes you against the wall. He is kissing you, touching you. You remember that he had beautiful hands. He has soft lips. You can feel his erection. You feel like you did when you were fifteen but when you were fifteen you would not have pushed back against that erection. It would have frightened you then. But what's frightening now is you. You raise your leg and circle his waist. You cannot get close enough.

There's a noise and the spell is broken. You push away and he follows you, he says your name over and over, but he, too, knows it is done. You go into your room and lock the door.

Your cellphone rings, again and again. It's him. You remember you gave him your business card. You should be more careful when you drink. He begins again, the litany. You hang up and he keeps calling. You're frightened now that you have met a madman. You are not laughing anymore. Finally, you say, "To-morrow," and set a time and he lets you be.

In the morning you meet your colleagues. They are lovely, educated, bright, involved, from all over the world. You are nervous about what has happened and afraid to be found out. You do your job and ignore the feeling between your legs that keeps coming unbidden. You are embarrassed by it but also stunned and somehow pleased.

He calls you that next night and you don't answer. He leaves a message that he will be there soon. He calls again to say he is there, waiting in the bar. He keeps calling but you don't answer and finally he stops.

You pretend he hasn't called and go about your business. He doesn't call again. The last night you have a farewell drink with your colleagues in the rooftop bar. It is very dark but still you are aware that he could be there. What would happen if he saw you? What could you possibly say? What would he do?

But you don't forget him and feel braver six thousand miles away. You tell your friends about it. Some of them think it's exciting. Most of them say it's no big deal. Let's be honest. You are a grown woman. You are not fifteen. What you don't tell them is that you didn't know you could feel fifteen again.

You are having another birthday and going back to work in that country, to stay at that very same hotel with the rooftop bar. You start to think, what the hell? You imagine the worst-case scenario . . . even being dead doesn't scare you.

In the middle of the night you dial the number, 971-507-734963. You still have it in your cellphone.

"I'm coming," you say when he answers, and you tell him the dates.

"I wait," he says.

The night before you leave the phone wakes you at 3:00 A.M. "Where are you?" he says.

It's a very long flight. You are more excited than frightened but more than that, you are determined and you call him when you arrive and say you will meet him in the bar. You are not sure what he looks like, not sure you will find him but very sure what you are doing. When before have you been the object of this passion? Maybe never, you think, never that you can remember.

You walk into the bar as awkward as the first time but you are looking as beautiful as it is possible for you to look. He sees you first, his shirt is as white as any *kandoora*, his eyes blacker than you remember.

You sit on a couch, you order a drink, he touches your neck, your arm, your leg. You're embarrassed that he is so young and that people will wonder what he is doing with you. You are wondering what he is doing with you.

You start to talk with a group of English girls sitting in the couches across from you. They are very young and blond with long bare legs, a bunch of girls who have come out from England to make their fortunes in this land of milk and honey where being white and English counts for something and you ignore this man who is looming over you. You take advantage of his imperfect English to establish your superiority.

But you are an asshole. He's not intimidated or embarrassed. He says later that they were coarse. You are taken aback because he is correct. You are realizing that he is dangerous when, after another drink, he says, "Let's go."

The elevator's empty and he kisses you against the wall and holds all the buttons so the elevator goes up and down and never stops. And you tell him then that he has to listen to you. He has to do what you ask and he is touching you and those black eyes are half-closed under those long black lashes and you know that you have no more chance than Saint Teresa against the angel.

You are terrified and so very hot.

"Give me ten minutes," you tell him.

Back in the room you don't know what to do. You get undressed because you don't want to be tangled in clothes but you don't want to be naked. You close the lights and open the curtains that look out on a construction site in the distance. You wait. It seems he is taking a long time.

There is a knock on the door and he backs you into the room. He kisses you and starts you up all over again. He starts to unbutton his white shirt. You stop thinking.

He is a little bit sweet, a little bit mean. He is a first-class lover. You have known men but you have never known anything like this. He doesn't ask and neither do you. You wonder about the things he doesn't do and if he would do them if you asked. You wonder about the things you would do if he asked, but he doesn't.

You think about the woman he will marry when he's forty. She'll be very young and most likely coveted. He will have a job and money to buy her a house and jewelry. His mother will choose her. Where is she now, this lucky girl? She will giggle about him with the other wives. And when they talk about the size of their husbands she will hold out her two hands and the wives will push at her shoulder and laugh. She will only have one child so her life will be easy.

You realize he does not want anything from you, just to be here in your bed. He leaves you spent. You carry him with you, your dirty secret. You sit and work but you feel like the cover of a dime-store novel. Your bodice has been ripped.

Still, you make him wait; one night he gets angry and doesn't come. One night you don't hear from him at all. You act like there will always be nights and play the game like you are fifteen. You are not thinking with your head.

He says he will see you before you leave. You meet him by the swimming pool in a green silk skirt. He liked a silk dress you once wore so you assume he likes silk. He has accused you of hiding him from your colleagues, and you have denied it, but it's true, which is why you are meeting him at the swimming pool, to prove your lie. It seems to you he will do anything you ask.

But tonight he's distracted. In the room he is rough and quick. Something you do annoys him. He gets a phone call. You can understand nothing. He tells you an elaborate story about having to go to the hospital. You sit up in bed like a wide-eyed child and he gives you a pity fuck. You are grateful and angry but you act neither.

"I am so sad," you tell him.

He is standing by the window, naked and young and cocky. "You made me cry a whole year," he says, not kindly.

"If you go," you say, "how will I find you?" You listen to yourself whine.

He grins. "But I can always find you," he says.

"I don't even know your name," you say, shocking yourself when you realize you don't know his name. You were determined to know nothing but now you want every detail. You want everything you can't have.

He is annoyed. "You know my name," he says, but you don't, you really don't, and he won't tell you. He's dressed and combing his hair in the mirror, so vain and rightly so. You don't want to get out of bed. You don't want to move. You want to remember him inside you and if you move it will go away like a vapor.

"Come back later, it doesn't matter what time," you say, and try to give him the key but he won't take it. He hesitates.

"Leave your phone on," he says, and lets you kiss him goodbye.

You lie awake with the cellphone on your pillow. At 4:00 A.M., you start to call him. It rings and rings but he doesn't answer. You curl into a ball in your bed for a day and a night. Your flight is at 2:00 A.M. You realize he is not coming back to you. And all your bravado is gone with him. You think crazy things. But you get on the plane and you go home.

You call him all the time. You call whenever you think of it. You call from work. You call from bed at night. It rings and rings. You look for someone to take his place. No one can take his place. You keep calling, convinced he is there but not picking up.

One day there's an answer. It's a recording and you listen closely. You hang on every word. *The cellphone number you have called has been switched off. Please try again later.*

It's a woman's voice. She says this in two languages. In English she has a lilting and pleasant British accent, as though she really does want you to try later.

You call the number for a year. You never go back to that country. You're never offered that job again. Still you call the number, as though calling were a job.

You make up stories about why he has switched off his phone. Sometimes you think he could be dead, killed crossing the border into Syria, or killed fighting against Assad.

Then, one day, the message changes. In her soft, lilting voice the woman with the British accent tells you that the cellphone number you have called is out of service. She doesn't tell you to try again. She is telling you it's finally over.

THE CHILD IN THE SUN

Mrs. Bubeneshwa lives in a house near Kalighat with a small child. Every day Mrs. Bubeneshwa sits the child in the sun on the back verandah and every day she rubs oil into the child's hair, oil the Tibetan woman in the market has sworn will turn brown to black, which is as it should be.

If you look closely at the child, if you look at the child for a long time, you will say there is something about the child. You will say that she does not belong here, but if you say this, Mrs. Bubeneshwa will make a hammock between her knees with the skirt of her sari and sit the child there, protectively.

"This is Chandra's motherless child," Mrs. Bubeneshwa will say to you, and touch her eyes with a clean white handkerchief that she has pulled from a pocket of fabric in her sari. But believe me, it's not the truth. Mrs. Bubeneshwa will not tell you the truth about the child.

"Chandra went to Switzerland," she will say. "She married there and had the child. Chandra was so light, so fair, that when she went to Switzerland, they did not believe she was from here." This is what Mrs. Bubeneshwa will tell you, but don't believe it.

· · ·

Julie rented a room from Mrs. Bubeneshwa. That's how they met. It wasn't a room the way you think of a room. It was a corrugated tin shed built on the roof of Mrs. Bubeneshwa's house. Inside the shed were shelves hung from the ceiling by ropes to foil the ants that would swarm up from the floor.

Julie would do morphine inside the tin shed. The crows would roost on the roof of the tin shed and make a racket and Julie would go outside and look down over the city, or sometimes she'd face in and look at the crows.

Mrs. Bubeneshwa didn't know what Julie was doing. She only knew that Julie was quiet, and when the afternoons got hot, and soot from the fires of the *bhar* wallahs blew onto the roof, Mrs. Bubeneshwa would invite Julie down into the house.

"How white you are," Mrs. Bubeneshwa would say, touching Julie's cheek. "I had a beautiful daughter once, fair like you." Julie was brown from the sun but Mrs. Bubeneshwa called her white.

Mrs. Bubeneshwa would wrap Julie in the saris that had, she said, belonged to Chandra, the daughter who went to Switzerland, and the two of them would lay across the wide rosewood carved bed on their stomachs, knees bent, bare feet in the air, and they would eat sweets soaked in honey and rosewater. The babu would bring them cups of hot milk tea. He would shell pistachios and Mrs. Bubeneshwa would feed them to Julie from her fingers. There were questions.

"Is it true," Mrs. Bubeneshwa would say, "that in your country the clothes of the master and the servant are washed in the very same pot?"

"It's true," Julie told her.

"And they eat from the very same dishes?"

"Yes," Julie told her.

"Another sweet?" Mrs. Bubeneshwa would say.

Mrs. Bubeneshwa liked Julie. Julie was beautiful and white, like Mrs. Bubeneshwa's daughter who had gone to Switzerland.

Brian went to India and he brought home a girl. Everyone said she was dark and must be an Indian. They are dark, you know. Brian brought Julie home to live in a house with his mother.

"She's very dark," Brian's mother said to him when Julie left the kitchen.

"She's Catholic," Brian said.

"I don't mind," his mother said, but there were questions.

"Tell me about the nuns," Brian's mother said, "and if it's true."

"Yes," Julie said, "the nuns, yes, it's true."

Julie left Brian and Brian's mother in Sydney and went to the house near Kalighat, and asked Mrs. Bubeneshwa if she could rent the room on the roof again. When she saw her, Mrs. Bubeneshwa said no, not necessary, and took her to stay in the wide rosewood carved bed downstairs.

When it was too hot at night Mrs. Bubeneshwa brought the mattress out on the back verandah and they would sleep there, the bamboo shades unrolled to keep out the morning sun. Mrs. Bubeneshwa fed Julie jhal muri and served her tamarind juice poured from a Waterford crystal pitcher that the shopkeeper in the market said had belonged to Queen Victoria. Mrs. Bubeneshwa brought her medicine from the Tibetan woman and English butter from the black market. She rubbed Julie's belly with perfumed oil.

Julie had the baby in the wide bed and Mrs. Bubeneshwa smudged *kajal* on the infant's forehead to keep her safe. "How white she is," Mrs. Bubeneshwa said, and fearful, she burnt chilies on a brazier. "The stinging smoke will blind the evil gods," she told Julie. "I did this also for my daughter Chandra, because she, too, was so beautiful, so white. The gods can be jealous."

When Julie left the house near Kalighat, she left the baby. Mrs. Bubeneshwa insisted and Julie had no defense. But not before six months had passed and the child could eat rice, not before the *annaprashan* ceremony. Mrs. Bubeneshwa insisted Julie stay until then and Julie had stayed. The day she left was the day the letter from Brian's mother arrived. Mrs. Bubeneshwa found it lying open on the hallway table where Julie had discarded it.

"I know what you've done," the letter said. "You are no better than the nuns."

Mrs. Bubeneshwa is sitting on the back verandah with the child. Mrs. Bubeneshwa sits in the shade of a black umbrella but the child she will tell you is her grandchild sits with her face turned up to the sun. Mrs. Bubeneshwa feeds the child shelled pistachios from her fingers.

"You are beautiful," she tells the child, "fair and white like your mother, your poor mother." In a pocket of fabric in her sari, Mrs. Bubeneshwa has a letter from her daughter in Switzerland.

"Dear Mummy," the letter says, "I hope you are well. I cannot come to see you. I could not stand the heat, the dirt. Switzerland is so clean, and white." Chandra's letters always say the same thing.

Mrs. Bubeneshwa will burn the letter the way she has burned the other letters. She will burn it in the afternoon when the sky is black with soot from the fires of the *bhar* wallahs. The sun is high now and Mrs. Bubeneshwa looks at it from under the black umbrella.

"Come here, my monkey princess," Mrs. Bubeneshwa says to the child, touching her cheek. "That's enough sun for today."

SUDDER STREET

Alberto took the money with him when he left. He took my friend Alice who lived in the room next door and whom I loved like a sister. He took the malaria pills, the mosquito net, and the plastic wheels of contraceptives I had carried all the way from Europe.

I went downstairs to tell Heidi who was lying on her bed drinking Romilar cough syrup. She was unimpressed when I told her what Alberto had done. She offered me the bottle of Romilar. She said it transformed reality and bestowed magical powers.

I had tried it once, late at night, in one of the world's deserts, the sky a dome of stars. "You'll see the future," he told me and I drank two bottles of the thick, sweet syrup meant to be taken in teaspoonfuls under clean sheets. That's all I remember.

"No one understands Romilar," Heidi said when I told her. "Romilar was meant to be sipped." She tipped the bottle back delicately and drank, then put it down on the floor near her bed. "Now what's the problem?"

"Alberto and Alice," I said.

"Don't live in the past," Heidi told me.

"But he took everything."

"You don't need that junk."

"What about money?"

"Sell something. There's always something to sell."

"What? You're not listening. There's nothing left."

"Nothing?" Heidi scoffed. "I don't believe it. There's no such thing. I'll have to come look for myself."

"What will I do?" I said. She fixed the pillow behind her head and folded her arms across her chest.

"Move in with me, of course."

Heidi had a room on the ground floor off the courtyard. Babu was standing out there now with piles of dirty sheets waiting for the rains so he could wash them, jump up and down on them, pound them with his feet until he decided they were clean.

Heidi got up from the bed and pulled me along with her. "Let's go," she said. "We'll get your things and move them down here before the rains start. We'll see what Alberto's left. There must be something. There's always something."

She stopped as she passed Babu standing on the dirty sheets to face him. She put her palms together, touched her forehead with the tips of her fingers and bowed. "*Namaste*," she said. Heidi stood six feet. She was magnificent; everything about her was oversized. Her dresses swept the floor. This one was green with red satin bands up the sleeves and at the hem. If her dress had had a train, I would have lifted it to my lips and carried it up the stairs.

Alberto despised Heidi. Alberto despised everyone. There was no one he spoke to at the hotel. He hadn't spoken to me since we arrived. The last time was at the train station when I hesitated about the rickshaw wallah pulling three times his weight up the incline of the Howrah Bridge.

"Get in," Alberto said. "This is his work. What do you know? Who are you?"

Easy for a prince, I thought. Spoken like a true prince, which Alberto was, the son of a Venetian prince, a descendent of the Doges. He had told me this himself. I got in the rickshaw. "Someone throws himself off this bridge every day," Alberto told me. That was the last time we spoke.

The room on the second floor where I had stayed with Alberto was small and dark. The twin beds were pushed together and the fan had been left on. It turned slowly and I pulled the string to make it go faster. Heidi was right. Alberto had not taken everything. Under the bed where we had slept were twelve volumes of Wilhelm Reich in Italian translation.

"Nice," Heidi said, picking up volume one, running her hand over the cover and along the spine. Then she found the box of telegrams. "What's in here?" Heidi asked me.

"Telegrams."

"It's locked," she said.

I shrugged.

"What do they say? Who are they from?"

"I don't know. They're Alberto's."

Since I had been with him, Alberto had received a telegram every day. Since we had been here, Babu would bring a telegram every day with the morning tea and every day Alberto would read the telegram, crush it in his fist until his knuckles went white and throw it across the room.

"*Porca Madonna*," he would say. He would pull his hair from the roots until his eyes bulged and then he would bend down, pick up the telegram, smooth it out across the top of his leg, and lock it into the box Heidi was holding in her hands. He carried the key in the pocket of his Italian army shorts.

Heidi sat down on the bed and tried to pry open the box. Finally, she smashed it on the floor. The telegrams flew everywhere. We picked some up. We let some fall to the floor and picked up others. They were all from Venice. They were all from Alberto's mother. They all said the same thing:

CARO TI PREGO VIENI A CASA STO MORENDO
MAMA

"It's his mother," I told Heidi. "She's dying and wants him to come home."

"Well, the box is worthless," Heidi said, "but you might get something for the books." I looked at her as though she had lost her mind.

"Wilhelm Reich?" I said. "In Italian?"

"You don't know very much for how long you've been here," Heidi said. "You don't seem to know anything. What's in them doesn't matter. They're beautiful books. They have red covers. They have gold edges. This is India. Try the money-changer."

"Tomorrow," I said, picking up the telegrams and smoothing them out across the top of my leg, pressing against the crease in the paper with the heel of my hand. I put them back into the box one by one.

Heidi put a hand on my hand. "You've got to get yourself together," she told me. She touched my cheek, then gathered up my things and walked out of the room just as the rains started.

I went to the desk out front to tell the hotel manager that I would be moving downstairs. The manager gave me the bill Alberto had left unpaid. I thanked him and said I would be back.

The next morning I brought the books to Salaam Rajah's stall in New Market and told him to make me an offer. Salaam

Rajah was reluctant although he could not deny the beauty of the bindings and the heaviness of the paper.

"Twenty rupees," he said.

"Salaam, please."

"Twenty-two."

I sat down on the bench meant for customers. The shop was small and cramped, filled with cheap tourist souvenirs, embossed leather purses and brass statues of the dancing Shiva, but Salaam Rajah was a rich man, a money-changer who gave twice the bank rate for American dollars and British pounds. Hard currency, he called it. Salaam Rajah was round and fat, with smooth dark skin, and oiled black hair, shiny like the back of a beetle. He seemed to take pity on me. His great brow furrowed.

"Won't you have a drink?" he said.

"Salaam, these books come all the way from Italy."

"England?"

"Italy. It's near England."

"Ah . . . ," he said. "But won't you have a lemon squash? A sweet lassi? A cup of milk tea perhaps?"

"Look," I said. "The pages have gold edges."

He picked up volume thirteen, titled *Cosmico Orgone Ingegneria*, and turned the book over in his hands. He ran a finger along the gold edges. I opened the book for him and showed him that even when lying flat, the gold was visible on the page. He began turning the pages with a wet thumb, creasing the paper, leaving soggy gray stains at the top corners as he went.

"I'll have a lassi," I said, hoping to distract him.

"Good. Yes. Excellent." He looked up, smiling. He called out to one of the small boys who waited outside the rows of shops to run errands and told him to bring a sweet lassi from the tea stall for the memsahib.

"I think fifty rupees is fair," I told Salaam Rajah. He stepped back from the counter and threw his hands in the air. He made clucking noises with his tongue. Sighing, he called me nearer. "I have two wives," he said, our faces close. "Always jealous, always wanting more. I have several children."

The boy arrived with the lassi in a handblown glass, chipped at the rim. Black specks floated on the surface of white foam and I twirled the paper straw until they disappeared. The straw had been reused too many times and unraveled as I put it to my mouth to take a sip. "Forty-five?" I said casually.

"Twenty-five."

I would not, I decided, carry nineteen volumes of Wilhelm Reich back to the hotel to lie in a heap on the floor. I cursed Alberto and his taste in books. I would throw the books in the street, I told myself, before I would take such a cheap price.

Confident, determined, insulted, I stood up from the bench and lined the books along the counter in numerical order from one to nineteen and I explained to Salaam Rajah that the numbers on the books were roman numerals. I did not bother to tell him that Rome was a city in Italy, that country near England.

"It's very sad for me to sell these books," I told him. "They are very rare and valuable and they belong in a fine house where everyone who comes in can see what an educated and cultured man lives there. That's why I would like you to have them, Salaam Rajah." I slurped the last of the lassi through the broken straw and put the empty glass on the counter. "They're yours for forty rupees."

Salaam Rajah tightened his mouth into a pleated line. He took something from his nose. I started to pack the books into my bag. I could hear the rain on the tin roof. The streets will be flooded by now, I thought.

"A pity, isn't it?" Salaam Rajah said. He shook his large head. He made his eyes sad. "You have carried these books so far. So many large books, so heavy, and now you must carry them back. It is very inconvenient for you, I'm afraid. I am feeling very badly about this."

I had three books in the bag. I dropped volume four. "Careful," Salaam Rajah shouted. "You will damage the bindings." He leaned over the counter and looked down as I picked up the book. "Let me see," he said. "Give it here." He inspected the corners. He ran his hand over the front and back covers. "I could give you twenty-eight," he said, "perhaps . . . thirty."

I reached out to pull the book from his hands but he was too quick and held it tightly to his chest. "Thirty-five, then," he said. His eyes narrowed as though he had surprised himself.

I emptied volumes one through three out onto the counter. "*Acha*," I said. We shook hands and Salaam Rajah unlocked his steel money box.

I tied the rupees into the edge of my lungi and tucked the knot at my waist. The small boys followed me through the market, pulling at my sleeves while the cloth merchants unrolled bolts of fabric in my path. For only a moment I thought of having a dress made, a green dress with red satin bands up the sleeves and at the hem but I passed through to the perfume sellers and bought instead a vial of jasmine oil, and outside at the flower sellers, a garland of frangipani for Heidi.

She was lying on her bed when I got back. She had gotten Babu to change the sheets. Babu did everything Heidi asked. His eyes followed her when she crossed the courtyard and before she even called out to him in the morning, he was at the door with tea and biscuits.

Heidi patted the edge of her bed for me to sit down and I put the garland of frangipani around her neck. I showed her the rupees I had gotten for Alberto's books. She touched my hair and said we would be good together. I would learn to take care of myself. She would teach me. We smoked a chillum with the doors shut so no one would come in and we slept through the afternoon heat and the rains.

When I paid Alberto's bill, the hotel manager gave me a telegram. It was from Venice, for Alberto, from his mother, and it said the same thing as all the others.

"She doesn't know he's gone," I told Heidi. "I guess he hasn't written to her yet."

Heidi made a bored face. "She'll find out soon enough," she said.

But the telegrams came every day for the rest of the week and the week after that. I opened each one and put it in the box. The telegrams I had received were smooth and neatly folded on top of the ones Alberto had crumpled and thrown across the room.

The city was getting hotter and more uncomfortable. Everyone who could leave had left. When it rained the sewers backed up and the streets disappeared under black water. Cows stood knee-deep in the black water eating the rotted vegetables that floated by. Government clerks walked to work with their trousers rolled and carried their socks and shoes in their hands. Memsahibs sat high in their rickshaws. The wallahs pulled the ends of their dhotis between their legs and tucked the edges in at their waists to keep them dry. Big insects flew into plates of food, cups of tea, faces.

In the afternoons, Heidi and I pushed the beds together under the fan. We took cold showers and lay wet and naked, side by side, and when the breeze from the fan had dried us, we went back into the shower. We did this until the heat of the afternoon had passed. Sometimes Heidi would turn and her hand would brush my hip, we lay so close together. I said Babu was peering at us through the slats of the door but Heidi said I was foolish.

An Indian man had come to the hotel one time. He had an expensive camera and asked if he could photograph us. There were a lot of us then, before the rains came, and he sat in a chair among the beds in the dormitory room and he took our pictures while we talked and smoked.

The next time he came he brought the pictures and showed me mine. I never looked at myself anymore. I had no mirrors and so I stared at the photos, at the shape of my nose, the line of my upper arm as I pushed back my hair. They were very good photos, I thought. I liked seeing myself. "Thank you," I said to him.

"Nothing," he said. "I am wanting to take more. But this time, perhaps, you could remove your clothing?"

Alberto said the Indians found us debauched and perverse, separated from our families, fornicators, never bearing children. He said they spied on us every chance they got. We were the ancient temple figures come to life. Alberto's small black eyes would dart back and forth trying to catch them. He would leap up suddenly and open the door when we were in the room upstairs and look for them but they were never there.

Heidi said she would get us out of the city but she needed time. It didn't matter to me. I was glad to be rid of Alberto and glad to be with Heidi in the room off the courtyard. In the evenings, Babu would bring us Chinese food from Mr. Fung's restaurant at the end of Sudder Street and we would eat sitting up in our beds. I only sometimes thought of Alice.

"There's more than this," Heidi said. "You settle too easily. That's why you end up with men like Alberto." Heidi promised we would go up to Nepal, to Kathmandu, and see the temples with carved wooden roofs. We would go over the bridge into Swayambhu and stand by the stone platform where the Tibetans left their dead for the vultures to devour. We would circle the Monkey Temple while the painted eyes on the temple doors watched over us.

"We'll take nothing with us," Heidi said. "They have beautiful velvet in Kathmandu. We'll have all new clothes, everything of velvet."

"Velvet trousers," I said.

"Velvet gowns," Heidi said.

"Velvet capes."

"Velvet hats . . . embroidered!"

"Do you think Alice's in Kathmandu?"

"If she is," Heidi said, "we'll find her."

She told me all this as we lay wet and naked under the ceiling fan in the afternoons and as we sat up in bed eating the Chinese food Babu had brought us from Mr. Fung's restaurant. "Something will happen," Heidi said. "It just takes time."

The telegrams from Alberto's mother kept coming. There was no more room in the box. I told Heidi that maybe I should write a letter to Alberto's mother and tell her that he was gone, that he had left with a girl named Alice whom I had loved like a sister. Heidi didn't answer.

But then a telegram arrived from Venice that was not from Alberto's mother, and it did not say the same thing as all the others. This one said:

FIGLIO DEVI RITORNARE A CASA
IMMEDIATAMENTE BIGLIETTO SEGUIRA
PAPA

I showed Heidi. "It's from his father. He's sending a ticket for Alberto to come home." Heidi emptied the Romilar bottle and asked me to put it outside the door for Babu who collected them and sold them to the used-bottle merchant in the bazaar.

I came back and sat on the edge of her bed. "Do you think his mother has died of grief?" I asked her.

"Oh," Heidi said. "I don't think people die of grief."

"Italians do," I told her. "Especially Italian mothers and absolutely over their sons." I knew more about some things than Heidi did. "What should we do?" I asked her. I wasn't learning to take care of myself, I realized. I needed Heidi. I listened to her make promises, waited for her to fulfill them.

"We do nothing," Heidi said, and patted the bed for me to come and sit beside her.

The ticket came in an envelope addressed to Alberto. It was hand-delivered by a postal clerk in a khaki uniform with high white socks and a red turban. There was a commotion in the courtyard when the postal clerk would not leave the envelope with Babu. "It is requiring a signature," the clerk insisted. Babu tried to wrench it from his hand; the clerk shouted.

I heard all this and opened the doors. When Babu saw me, he let go of the envelope and ran over. "Letter, memsahib, letter," he said. And to the clerk, "Give the memsahib her letter."

The postal clerk held the letter out to me, out of Babu's reach. "Give it over," Babu said to the clerk. "Memsahib gets a telegram every day. This is only a letter and you are causing such a fuss."

"Special delivery," the clerk said, "a special delivery letter."

I signed Alberto's name and took the envelope. Babu followed me back to the room and was angry when I gave the postal clerk four anna. I gave Babu four anna as well and he left, a little less angry.

I took the envelope in to Heidi who was lying on her bed. Inside the envelope was a first class ticket, Calcutta to Venice via New Delhi and Rome. The date was open. It had been paid for in what Salaam Rajah called hard currency. Heidi held it up in both her hands. She flipped the thin carbon pages. Her eyes opened up as though she could see the future. "Our ticket out," she said to me.

I took the ticket from her hands. "We can't use this ticket," I said. "It's in Alberto's name. It's a ticket to Venice. Alberto's father sent it. Alberto's father is a prince. Didn't I tell you that?"

"This is India and Europe is full of princes," Heidi said. "For how long you've been here you don't know very much."

I gave her the ticket and sat down on the bed next to her. "Teach me," I said. She put my hand inside her blouse. Her breasts were round and heavy.

"Trust me," she said. "We've got our ticket out." She guided my fingers to where I could feel her heartbeat. "That's an American expression, isn't it?" she said. "Ticket out?"

Heidi dressed carefully to go to New Market to see Salaam Rajah. She wound a blue silk sari over a green satin petticoat. Her blouse was short and tight and showed her midriff, the skin pale and smooth. She slipped bangles up both her arms. She drew around her eyes with kohl and stained her lips with red powder she had bought in a stall near Chowringhee. I braided a gold ribbon in her hair and she looked so beautiful, so power-ful, that I almost fainted and had to sit down on the bed.

I watched her paint a blue dot in the center of her forehead. "Wish me luck," she said when she left.

"Good luck," I said, and thought about her never coming back.

The sun came through the slats in the door. I sat on Heidi's bed until the room was dark and the courtyard was quiet. There was only the sound of the fan. Babu had taken up his place in the chair at the entrance to the hotel, outside the courtyard. At night, he was the watchman. I stared at the ceiling and imagined monsters and gods in the water stains left by the monsoon rains. I closed my eyes and thought about the person who that day had jumped off the Howrah Bridge into the Hooghly River.

In the morning Babu came to the door with two cups of milk tea and four biscuits. I took the tray inside. He pushed his head between the slatted doors looking for Heidi. "She's not here," I told him. He bowed and as he backed down the step into the courtyard, I regretted that I had exposed him.

I drank my tea and the tea meant for Heidi. I looked around the room to see what I had been left with this time. In the corner of the room was a tin trunk where Heidi kept her things. It was painted with pictures of the Hindu gods: Krishna, Ganesha, Hanuman. Kali, the black goddess of destruction, was painted on the lid. I counted the human heads in her necklace before I opened the trunk.

Inside were Heidi's extravagant dresses, a bottle of Romilar, and some ten-rupee notes. I put on the green dress with the red satin bands up the sleeves and at the hem.

When it was dark I took the money and the bottle of Romilar and got into a rickshaw at the end of Sudder Street. I took the rickshaw to Kalighat.

In the Kali temple, I gave the priest the rupees from Heidi's trunk. I sat before the image of the goddess of creation and destruction, stained red with the blood of sacrifices, and I sipped the Romilar until the bottle was empty, until I had magical powers, until I saw the future.

ACKNOWLEDGMENTS

Black Warrior Review: "Sudder Street"

The Malahat Review: "Where It Belongs," under the title "United States of America"

Prairie Winds: "A Child in the Sun"

River Styx: "Mother Love"

StoryQuarterly: "Six and Five"

"Fish Heads" appeared in *A Fork in the Road: Tales of Food, Pleasure, and Discovery on the Road*, ed. James Oseland (Lonely Planet, 2013).

"Death Becomes Her" appeared in *For Keeps: Women Tell the Truth about their Bodies, Growing Older, and Acceptance*, ed. Victoria Zackheim (Seal Press, 2007).

"James Dean and Me" appeared in *Mondo James Dean*, eds. Lucinda Ebersole and Richard Peabody (St. Martin's Press, 1996), under the title "No-Man's Land."

"Sister-in-Law" appeared in *Staten Island Noir*, ed. Patricia Smith (Akashic Books, 2012).

Thanks to the friends and family, to the Ucross Foundation and the American Academy in Rome, and especially to Sarah Gorham, for her vision and unparalleled editing.

LOUISA ERMELINO is the author of three novels: *Joey Dee Gets Wise*, *The Black Madonna*, and *The Sisters Mallone*. She lives in New York City.

SARABANDE BOOKS is a nonprofit literary press located in Louisville, KY, and Brooklyn, NY. Founded in 1994 to champion poetry, short fiction, and essay, we are committed to creating lasting editions that honor exceptional writing. For more information, please visit sarabandebooks.org.